EDWIN
GRIFFIN BROTHERS BOOK 1

KATHI S. BARTON

This is a work of fiction. Names, characters, places, and incidents are products of the author's imagination or are used fictitiously and are not to be construed as real. Any resemblance to actual events, locations, organizations, or persons, living or dead, is entirely coincidental.

World Castle Publishing, LLC
Pensacola, Florida

Copyright © Kathi S. Barton 2021
Paperback ISBN: 9781955086936
eBook ISBN: 9781955086943
First Edition World Castle Publishing, LLC, September 20, 2021
http://www.worldcastlepublishing.com

Licensing Notes

Cover: Karen Fuller
Editor: Maxine Bringenberg

Prologue

Charles—Charlie, to most people who knew him—was so lost he hadn't any idea if he was walking on the ground or the sky. He knew the difference, of course, but it was so dark out tonight that if there had been a moon shining, he couldn't see it. When he sat himself down on a log to get his bearings again, he paused in his thinking to look at what could have made the sound he'd heard.

Terrified out of his mind when he saw glowing eyes looking at him, Charlie sat as still as he could. The eyes grew larger and incredibly more shiny as the beast made its way to him. He didn't run, knowing that even if he knew where he was at the moment, the wolf would know it better. It would chase him down and kill him without any hesitation.

The wolf, a big gray fella, just stood there within a few inches of Charlie's outstretched legs. When he laid down, putting his heavy head onto his leg, Charlie had another moment of fear. The thing never took his eyes off him. As soon as he felt he was brave enough to try and talk to the wolf, he was gone, and in his place was a man. A fully clothed man with the gray of the wolf's fur colored into his hair. Even his eyes were the same as the wolf's, Charlie thought. Still, neither of them moved until the man sat back on his butt and regarded him.

"You live on the property not far from here, is that correct?" Charlie told him he was only squatting there until they found him. But he was a mite lost. "Yes, I've been following you for some time. And in all that time, you did not harm any other animal you came across, and there were plenty. Why is that?"

"You mean the rabbit and the family of deer?" The man nodded. "I don't have a need for meat just now. I only kill when I have to. When my belly feels like it can't go another minute without some meat in it. And even then, I use it up the best I can. What I can't use, I leave out for some other animal that will use the rest. Why do you ask?"

"I'll get to that. You didn't seem that surprised when I changed from wolf to man. Can you tell me why that is?" He nodded and told him what he'd been seeing a lot of lately. "Yes, wars — including the current Comanche War — have made a man wish for better times. So you were surprised but just wrote it off as being another strange thing that had no explanation. That's a very good explanation, I think."

"They say that the war is about over. I don't know much about that. I can still hear shooting when I'm out and about. I don't have any land left because the soldiers took it all when they was coming through. Not that it was much more than a bunch of rocks and stumps, to begin with." The man only nodded. "I'm Charles Griffin. Most call me Charlie. A great deal more names, but I ignore them. Not everybody was able to go to school all the time. I had my family to feed when my daddy up and got sick. Momma died a few weeks ago, and I've been roaming around since looking for work. I don't suppose you know anyone around here that might be wanting an extra hand or two, do you?"

"I do, as a matter of fact. My name is Romeo Hank. The Hank is for when I need a last name.

But I do have something I'd like to propose to you if you've got the time to listen." Charlie told him he didn't have anything but time right now. "All right. I have a medium sized pack. You can see a few of them over there watching over us. They're all just wolves. I'm the only wolf shifter I know. They're a good bunch. Hungry most of the time, but then all of us are, correct?"

"Yes. Some more than others. At least I can find me a bit of string and fashion me up a hook to use." Romeo told him that was excellent. "You need me to fish some fish out for you and your pack? I don't mind at all doing that for you. In fact, I'd be powerful happy to help you out."

"Not just yet. But I think I will take you up on it soon. I have a daughter. Her name is Luna. Such a beautiful name, don't you think?" Charlie asked if it meant moon. "It does. Thank you. You're very well educated for a man with no means of living."

"My mom was a school teacher when I was born. They fired her, of course, when she had me. She taught me to read and to figure. I can write too, but I do have to think about the spelling of things. Can you write?" Romeo said he'd been given a great gift in that. "I think so too. When I find me a newspaper or some little old book, I treasure it for a bit. Then I pass it on if I can. I don't have to know the people in the paper. I just like reading about their stories. Are you going to tell me what this is about?"

"I am. I was working up to it, but I believe you to be a man that can be trusted with things in life. I would like to change you into a wolf, one such as I am. You'll be a man when you wish, a wolf when necessary. There will be magic, as well as wealth." Charlie told him he didn't have use for wealth, but food all the time would be nice. "That is precisely what I'm speaking about, Charlie, my good man."

Throughout the rest of the night and well into the morning, they spoke of things that Romeo needed from him. It wasn't brought up again about him being changed, but Romeo did tell him more about his daughter and that he, plain old Charlie, was her mate. The soul reason he'd not been harmed while wandering around in the woods.

"Do you understand what it is I want you to do?" Charlie said he thought so. "No. I'm sorry, I can't allow you to go into this, only thinking you understand. Please, ask me anything you'd like. You must be clear on this. I need you to be clear on how it is I wish you to someday take over for me."

Romeo never got upset with him when he asked his questions. If Charlie was honest with himself, which he usually tried to be, he was afraid that Romeo had picked the wrong man. That he'd be better off finding himself someone else to take over his empire.

"You're the right man, Charlie. When I told you I'd been following you around, I want you to know it wasn't just last evening, but for some time now. I've seen you share your last bit of food with people. Work for someone that cannot do for themselves and not take anything but a bit of bread and water. You're a very good man. A better man than I am." Charlie started to protest. "No. I'm correct in picking you as my replacement. And if that is some of your worry, being an alpha, you've no worries there either. I will not leave this earth for the next until you are comfortable with what is needed of you. Now. If you've no more questions, I shall leave you to allow you to think on it. I'll be back here tomorrow so you can tell me your answer. I know I have picked the right man, Charlie. It's something you can do easily to save this pack and my daughter."

Luna followed him as he walked around.

He'd thought about calling back Romeo and asking more questions, but he didn't. Sitting down again, his leg bothering him from sitting so long, he looked at the big, beautiful wolf.

"You're not really his daughter, are you?" She shook her head. "I didn't think so. Are there any more of the others that he claims are his children?" She nodded this time, and he determined by asking questions that it was one other female. "I don't know what to think about all this, to be honest with you. Are you my mate? Is he telling me the truth? I just don't know what to think."

She nodded or shook her head after each of the questions he put to her. Yes, she was his mate. Yes, Romeo was telling the truth. There were many more questions and answers.

He was headed back to the area that he'd first seen Romeo when he felt the pain take his breath away as it slammed into his left shoulder. Falling back, he hit his head and laid there while trying his best to catch his breath. That was when he heard the other gunshots, the wolves howling and trying to hide. Pulling Luna toward him, he whispered harshly into her ear, hoping that at least she'd understand him enough to know that she must warn the others.

"Go. Tell Romeo to hide the pack. To make sure you and your sister are safe." She didn't want to leave him, whimpering at him as she laid her head on his shoulder. "Go. Please. Run and escape before they hurt you too."

When she left him, Charlie closed his eyes. Opening them when he felt the shadow darken over him, he looked up in time to see the barrel of a large rifle. He was a goner. He knew that. He could only hope that Luna and the others were safe.

Chapter 1

Present Day

"You've never been one for parties, have you, son?" Edwin winked at his mom and hugged her tightly. "However, in this, I'm ever so happy that you decided to invite your dad and me to come. It's not every day that a man retires from the army as a command sergeant major. My goodness, I'm so very proud of you. My oldest boy, a major. However, it's hard to believe others could understand how a man who looks as young as you could make it to that rank. Do they?"

"Thanks, Mom. I feel good about it too. And since I ranked so high—you're right, being an immortal took care of it so I could—others believe it, and I'm taken care of for the rest of my life too." With a quick hug, she moved away from him when the commander in chief came to shake his hand. He asked what his plans were now. "I'm going to go home when my parents do and try to maybe sleep past five in the morning a couple of times. I might come to like that too."

They both laughed, knowing full well he'd not be able to sleep late. "Have you given any thought to what I talked to you about a few days ago? The recruiting offices could use a good role model like you hanging around." Edwin told Mr. President that he didn't want to make any decisions for a few more months. "I understand that. When my term is up in another three years, I'm going to try and be a man of leisure myself. I don't know how that will set with my wife. Emma has a list as long as I am of things she wants to get done. I thought for sure that being the president would have her cutting me some slack, but alas, it didn't."

Mingling around with the president, Edwin was glad he was able to introduce his parents to the man. He was a nice guy. Polite. But Edwin had never cared for his wife. Too many dealings with her, he supposed, to form a positive opinion of her.

She'd been caught out too many times by a patrol and had to be taken home. Drunk and disorderly hadn't been nearly enough for her. No. Emma was nasty and a mean drunk. Not only that, but she wasn't a quiet one either, shouting to whoever would listen about who she was and how unsatisfying Mike was to her sexually. Edwin didn't like her at all.

At one in the morning, things began to break up. If he'd had any say about it, he would have left hours ago, but his parents were having a wonderful time, and he just couldn't say no to them. Going back to the hotel where they were staying, his dad caught him just as he was going out the door.

"You're not going back, are you, Edwin?" He told his dad that he was finished. "Good. There is no reason for you to be around when things start to hit the fan. And they will, as I've told you boys before."

"I know, Dad. I don't know whether to be glad for that second site of yours or think it's a curse. It's nothing I'd want to have." Dad just stared at him for a moment before Edwin turned away. "Dad, you know I don't use anything like that anymore. Not only is it too dangerous, but it's difficult to explain where I might have gotten the information. It's just easier to let things go where they roll."

"It is. But not where my family is concerned."

Hugging his dad, Edwin went to the room across the hall from them. Not that he had lied to his dad, but he figured he was better off telling his dad what he wanted to hear rather than the truth. Not only could Edwin see a great deal into the future, but it had made them very wealthy over the years and had saved his brothers from being hurt quite a few times as well. But the most important thing he'd been able to do was to save himself quite a bit of trouble as well.

Lying on his bed, Edwin thought about what his life was going to be from here on out. Not having any plans wasn't helping him. He already had a home he could move right into. A car sitting in the garage that Dad had told him he'd had serviced just a few days ago. Also, he had a part-time job that he was actually looking forward to working at.

He and Garfield had been best friends since his little brother began to talk. Not that either of them were all that talkative, but when either of them had something to say, they said it and were quiet again. Edwin could spend hours with Garfield, and the two of them wouldn't say a word. It was just how he liked it. Garfield too.

Getting up, knowing he wasn't going to sleep, Edwin pulled out his computer. Three days ago, he'd turned it over to be cleaned. When he'd gotten it back, not only hadn't anything been taken off of it, but there were more programs, as well as icons than there had been. Opening up one of them now after making sure he was offline, Edwin read over the files in the first folder.

Nothing too big. A few menus for some upcoming dinners at the State House. There was a list of the people working them and their levels of clearance. There was even a notation by some of the names and their allergens. The president was allergic to peanuts. He'd not known that.

As he went through each file, careful to keep checking for any kind of trouble, he was just about to close up one of the last two files when the hotel phone rang next to the bed. Getting up to answer it, he paused just before touching it when his extra senses seemed to tingle just a little. Moving back to his seat, he sat there staring at the phone as it continued to ring for several minutes. When it stopped, Edwin touched his finger to the phone handle and closed his eyes. Reaching beyond this room and to the switchboard area in the hotel, the magic led him out of the hotel to the high hanging lines above the city.

Following the current that ran along the phone lines—he always thought this was one of the stupidest gifts he'd been given, to be able to trace a current from a phone call to him. He'd never tried doing it for someone else, too embarrassed to find out what might be on the other end of the line.

By the time he was at the phone where the call had originated, Edwin could only stare at the people sitting around the room. Of the nine people in the room, he knew only two of them. One of them was Mike, the other Vice-President Jamison Current. The men were drinking beers, it looked like to him, as well as smoking big cigars. They were staring at the phone as if they were expecting something to happen to it.

"He said he'd think about it, but I know he's going to turn it down. Edwin is a good man, too good to be sitting in a recruiting office for us." Jamison nodded but didn't speak when Mike did. "What makes you think he's going to want to work for us after this? We can't have him out in the open. He'll stick out like a sore thumb. I've never seen anyone as built like he is and still able to eat like he's never getting another meal."

"I told you why, you idiot." Jamison looked around the room, then leaned closer to Mike. "He's not human. I know we can't ask that of our men nowadays, but I know for a fact that he's not even close to being like us. And he'll do the job we need him to do, or we'll have to go to the next level. Griffin is the only one that will be able to fall from grace with this and not have it come back on the two of us."

Edwin didn't know what was going on, but he was sure it had nothing to do with him being a recruiter for the army. As it was right now, he most assuredly wasn't taking the job. One of the other men came to hand something to Jamison, who then handed it off to Mike.

"So? He's gone back to his hotel and didn't leave again. What does that have to do with anything?" Jamison told Mike that he had a tracker on Edwin. "What sort of tracker? And why the hell would you do that? Do you want him to catch us? Jesus H. Christ, Jamison, you're stupid if you think he's just going to let it go if he finds it on his person."

"He won't. I have ways that will even astound you about getting those little suckers where no one will find them. They're so little nowadays that I was able to get one made into an aglet." Mike looked confused. "The little tip at the end of a shoe lace. Don't you ever do crossword puzzles? I've had them put on each and every pair of his shoes that he had in the service. We both know he won't toss anything away until it's worn out completely. This will let us keep an eye on him and know when he comes back around. Trust me when I tell you, we're going to dig up so much shit on that boy that it'll be easy to convince him to work with us again. On the sly, too."

Edwin thought of the shoes he had with him and the few pair he'd been meaning to send home. He was going to get rid of them all as soon as possible before he went back to his house. As the men talked about the upcoming dinner they were hosting, as well as ad campaigns, he looked around the room. Going back to keep checking on the two most powerful people in the United States, he learned very little from the other guests.

When he was able to leave the room they were in, Edwin thought about what he'd learned. Basically nothing. He was going to be the fall guy for something the two of them were planning. They needed to keep track of his every move, and — this bothered him the most — they thought him to be very stupid. Perhaps he had been, but he wasn't now.

When the phone rang again, he felt the familiar vibrations of his parents and picked up the phone. Deciding it was time he came clean with them, Edwin would tell them on the plane. But not where there could be anyone around to overhear him. Instead, he decided to meet his parents for breakfast in the hotel and leave all the trouble brewing for later.

"I, for one, am thrilled to be going home." He told his mom he was looking forward to it as well. "I'm so glad to hear that. While I don't have any plans for you this summer, I would like to make up for lost time and visit with you a good deal more. Your brothers are home as well now. Even Jeffery."

Jeffery had been away most of his life. While Edwin had been in the army, Jeffery had gone on to be one of the best kept secrets in the world. He was a satellite engineer and could take a picture of a person several thousand miles away and tell you what their shit looked like. He was fond of telling them that. He went by the name "Junkie," and not even the president knew they were related, nor where Jeffery hung his hat. He was that good.

Tony, his brother and litter twin who had been born when he had was an electrical engineer. There hadn't been anything made that he couldn't take apart and put back together better. He could wire up a house so it used little to no electricity, as well as tweak an engine, so it ran better than anything on the market. Smiling to himself, he thought of all the trouble the two of them had gotten into as boys growing up, just by taking things apart and seeing how easy they could tweak it when put back together.

Garfield was the quiet one, but he was also the smartest man he knew, besides their dad. Perhaps it was magic or something more, but Garfield could take a penny and make it into hundreds of dollars in very little time. That was another thing that had made them very wealthy. The way the two of them knew just what to invest in and exactly when to pull out or sell something that was going to take a dive.

Harman, second from the youngest, seemed to be adrift most of the time. Not that he wasn't busy — he was that and more. But Harman had his hands into a great many things going on. He'd written several books on different subjects, from flower gardens to the volcanic ash that still fell to the ground and its effect on the earth. He'd been an oceanographer as well as a zoo keeper. Harman was a man you went to when you had a question about any subject you could think about. He was also a killer at crossword puzzles.

Then there was his brother Stone. The youngest of all of them, Stone had been born a lone pup. Good thing too, Mom always said, as he was the largest by far. Each of them had weighed about three pounds when they were born, bigger than a regular wolf pup by double. But Stone had weight seven pounds. For all his size and muscle, he was a kindergarten teacher at the local elementary school. Stone was well-loved by all his students, as well and the unmarried and married parents.

As soon as he disembarked from the plane, he was engulfed in big strong arms. It wasn't as if he'd not been home in the last twenty some years, but now that he was home for good, his brothers welcomed him in the best way possible. Even Mom and Dad, who had hugged him a great deal over the last few days, joined in the fun.

Did you do what I asked you to do with the shoes? Nodding at Jeffery, Edwin handed him the suitcase that was lined with a lead box with his shoes in it. *Good. I'll take care of this when I get back home. Also, I'm going to have you guys run through a couple of other pieces of equipment that I have so I can get rid of any bugs or other shit you might have picked up.*

Do you think that's necessary? Jeffery told him it was always necessary when dealing with the government. *I suppose you're right. I told Mom and Dad what I knew and could do. I thought they'd be upset with me, but they don't seem to be anything but proud that I was able to take care of myself while away.*

As they should be. I'll get back to you with the information. In the meantime, come by the house, and we'll get you guys cleaned up.

They rode to his house in a rental even though they all had cars, just to be sure it was clean too.

Christ, Edwin thought. It was only his first day home, and he was already feeling like he'd never be clear of the shit of the government.

~*~

Rain hated to stand in line at the grocery. Not to mention, just being away from home, period. It wasn't like she couldn't leave. Rain just hated to be outside her comfort zone. She'd been working from home for the last decade and didn't see any reason for that to change now.

Looking around, she saw her sister Storm walk into the store with a cart. Rain loved her sister, but she was also afraid of her. Not that she'd hurt her or anything, but Storm was a great deal like her name. A storm to be afraid of.

The cashier slapped her hand on the belt, and it startled her enough to bring her out of her thoughts. "Are you high or something? I said to put your stuff up here. I'm not going to do it." The man behind her inhaled sharply, and Rain was just about to leave when Storm stood in front of her cart. "Christ, will you get your head out of your ass before I have to have you kicked out?"

"Carl!" Storm yelled loudly, and the cashier told her to shut up. "I will not shut up, you overweight pig. What gives you the right to talk to someone like that? Carl? You're needed on lane six."

"You fucking bitch. What do you think he's going to do? Huh? He's my dad, and he'll bar you from here before he will do anything to me. You remember that when he tells you to get out of here." Carl showed up, and Storm explained to him, in a very calm, scary voice, what the woman had done to her sister. "No, I didn't. She was just standing here with her eyes all glazed over like she was high or something. I don't have time for that sort of crap going on around here, Dad. I didn't do anything wrong. It was all this woman here."

Rain wanted to climb into a tree and never get out. Instead, she stood still when Storm moved the cart and held her hand. The yelling back and forth was making her ill. Her body seemed to be turning inside out when suddenly she was sitting on a seat with her head between her knees.

"Just keep breathing, honey. You'll be just fine." She didn't know the man holding her in the position, but since she could still hear Storm yelling at Donna—she'd only just discovered the cashier's name—Rain was all right. When she lifted her head up, she stared at the man in front of her. "My name is Charlie Griffin. That your sister? I've seen her around town a bit. Not so much you."

"Yes. She's always been my best defender. I have trouble with people. I'm fighting daily to get out and about." They both watched as Carl tried to talk over his daughter when she began telling him she was going to tell her mom. "In a minute or two, Storm is going to be fed up with her and pull her gun out. It'll be all over the paper how she had to murder a cashier for her little sister."

The man laughed and sat down beside her before speaking. "It's good to have someone in your corner all the time. I have me the same trouble when it comes to being around crowds of people. I was such a loner after the war." She didn't think he looked old enough to fight in the last war, but she kept her mouth closed. "There she goes. You hit that one right on it. I would have thought there wasn't any way she could be carrying a gun in here."

"She's retired military. She did or sometimes does reconnaissance work for them. Not really retired, I guess. Storm helps them once in a while when they need someone smart and mouthy." They both laughed this time. "Carl has his hands full with Donna. I almost feel sorry for him."

"I told him some time ago that she was going to be trouble for him. He needed to discipline her more. Went in one ear and right out the other. Oh well, you reap what you sow, I guess." Mr. Griffin got up when Carl called for someone to call the police. "I'd better make myself known here. Just you sit right here, child.

I'll make sure you're not going to be blamed for any of this."

Mr. Griffin only had to make himself seen by Carl before things started to calm. Well, for the store manager and his daughter, anyway. Storm still had her gun in her hand, but at least she wasn't pointing it at anyone right now. When she suddenly turned and looked at her, Rain wondered what had happened and felt her body tense up. Looking around, she saw the two people coming toward her, and Rain made her way to her sister.

"Don't say a word." She shook her head as she held onto Storm. "Remember, they can't hurt you anymore, Rain. I've got this. All right?"

"Yes. All right. Don't leave me with them, Stormy. Please?" She said she'd never do that. Her parents had done more things to her as a child than anyone knew, with the exception of her sister. "What do they want?"

"I'll find out. You just keep right here close to me — or better yet, go hide." Mr. Griffin took her other hand, and she held onto it like a lifeline. "Mr. Griffin, if you could please take my sister to the office and stay with her, I'd very much appreciate it."

"I can do that, but I'd rather stick right

here next to you. Go on now, Rain. You go on to the office and stay there. If Carl is in there, you lock the door and don't come out until Stormy here, or me come to get you."

She didn't want to go, but their parents were getting closer. Turning quickly, she did just what she was told and made her way to the office.

Her parents being here at this time couldn't have been a coincidence. Them showing up right now was just the sort of scene they would live for. Either they'd been looking for her and Storm, or they had been out looking for them and happened to see them in the store. Whatever it was, Rain was afraid.

When she and her sister were little, their parents would parade them around like they were some sort of freak show. Stormy could remember anything and everything. Not only that, but she could recall details that would never be seen by anyone else in the room. It was what had made her a good soldier.

Rain could make a computer do things it shouldn't. Not that she knew the first thing about programming it or even how to turn it on back then. But with a small touch to the screen, she could bring up any information ever stored on one. Neither fire walls nor passwords slowed her either.

Since growing older, her skills had improved a great deal. So had Storm's. The two of them could and did hack into things that saved a great deal of money for a lot of people. Even offshore accounts could be emptied in no time. Bank accounts that she'd set up would never show up on a bank audit. Then when the time was right, Rain and Storm would distribute the money to charities all over the world, and no one ever knew it was the two of them.

"Rain? It's Storm. Can you let me in?" She got up to get the door unlocked and opened it enough for her sister to slip in. "They're still here. Mr. Griffin is going to take you out the back way to his home for a few hours. I'm pressing charges against Donna, then going to see what the hell our parents want. Did you know they were back?"

"No. I've not spoken to them since forever." Storm nodded and paced the tiny office. "I should have stayed home today. But I was out of everything."

"You need to get out more, honey. You know that. But I would like it if you were to call me the next time you go out. Especially with them around. Mom has some fresh bruises, and Dad has tried to cover up a black eye with makeup. I wonder if he realizes how stupid he looks doing that. Whatever they want, it's more than likely money. You not only watch for them, Rainyday, but you also keep an eye out for anyone that might be stalking you. They've more than likely told someone that we're going to get them whatever it is they want from Mom and Dad."

"The last time they were in town was ten years ago. Remember?" Of course, she did, and Stormy asked her if she'd been contacted by them in any way. "No. Not once. I have been keeping tabs on them as you said to do, but I sort of let that go when I thought they were going to jail for a while. I wonder how they managed to get out."

"I don't know, but I intend to find out. Will you go home with him?" She said she would if Storm were to come there too. "I will if only to get you. We'll stay at my house. You can handle that, can't you? For a few days? I don't want to stress you out."

"No. I can stay there. I'd like that." Storm nodded, then hugged her. "Stormy, I have to tell you about where I'm living. It's not a good place."

"I've seen it. I'm hoping that once I get you

out of there for a while, you'll stay with me for good. We could have some fun together." Rainy wasn't one to cry a great deal, knowing that tears were useless. But she did cry then, holding onto her sister tightly as she did so. "Rainy-day, you'll be fine. Mr. Griffin is a good man, you know that. Just go there with him and do what he tells you. He also knows you're going to need to be alone. He's a wolf — you knew that, didn't you?"

"Yes. All of his family is. All right. I'll wait here for him. But you have to promise me you'll be careful with them around." She promised her she would. "Then later, I'll go and get my clothing from the place I'm staying and not go back. If you're sure about me living with you."

"I'm very sure. All right. Mr. Griffin will knock, and you go with him." When Storm left the little office, she returned before the door closed completely. "I know how you feel about guns, but I want you to carry this until I see you. I'd feel better if you could protect yourself in the meantime."

She took it without hesitation. That seemed to make Storm feel better, so she let out a long breath. As soon as Mr. Griffin showed up, he took her out the front door without anyone noticing them. Rain hoped that no one had seen them anyway.

They drove by her home, and Mr. Griffin pulled into the drive. He looked at the place, then at her, before he backed out of the drive. She knew what the place looked like. It was little more than a few walls put up under a leaking roof and broken windows. But at the time, she'd not been able to afford anything else. Then it got to the point where she couldn't leave without having a panic attack.

"You'll need some new things after this." She told the man she was going to live with Storm. "Might do you both some good to be doing that. That place there is a terrible place for a pretty woman to be living. Even if you was ugly, which you ain't, I'd not want you living there. Should have been torn down years ago."

"It worked for me. That's all I needed at the time." He nodded, seeming to understand more than Stormy did. "Mr. Griffin, did Storm tell you about our parents? About why I'm hiding from them?"

"She didn't have to. They made it clear when they came into the store that they'll be wanting you to do some tricks for them. I'm assuming they think you owe them or something?" She told him it was something like that. "Well, I'm right proud of you both for not doing a thing they want. They'll see themselves back in prison before too long if they keep hounding the two of you like they are. Or that Stormy will kill them. Either way, they need to back off."

"I think that's an excellent plan. However, it rarely works out for us. They've never beaten us or anything like that, but they do have a way of making our lives very difficult when it comes to trying to make a living." Mr. Griffin told her his family would help. "You've done more than enough already. I'm just so glad you were there for me today. I don't know what I would have done had you and Stormy not shown up."

"You would have done just fine."

She wasn't so sure but didn't say anything more.

As soon as they pulled up in front of his home, she knew she'd be safe there. Six big men were standing there on the porch, each of them looking like they could stand up to just about anything. She hoped so. If her parents found them, they'd make these people wish they'd never stepped in where lesser men had walked away.

Chapter 2

"You must be Storm." Storm looked at the woman sitting in a rocker on the front porch. "My boys are in the house. Your sister had to lie down. It was a tad too much for her to be around all of them at one time. Has she always been this timid?"

"More so since she's been on her own. Mostly she stays at home, never leaving until she needs something. However, I'm not sure I'd call her timid so much as I'd call her overwhelmed. She'll get better around all of them when she gets to know them better. Not that I foresee that happening—we're not exactly the type of people that get invited to homes like this one. No offense toward you. However, I'm not going to allow anything to happen to her." She nodded.

"You're Mrs. Griffin."

"Luna. My husband is Charlie. Please call us that. While I'm not sure what you meant by not being invited to houses like ours, I want you to know that you are very welcome here. Anytime you wish to come." Storm didn't comment either way. "Come have a seat. Dinner will be ready soon enough, and we can get to know each other. My son, Edwin, he retired just the other day from the army. The others, they live around here too, but they came here to be with him for a few hours. It's a lot for me, and I raised them. What is it you do that makes you magical? I know you have a good deal of it. Magic, I mean. What is it from?"

"From? I don't know. I've always had it. Rain too." She nodded as if she knew that. "We don't talk about it much with strangers. People tend to want tricks from us, and we're not doing those anymore."

"I've heard about the incident at the grocery. My husband let me know about your parents. I would expect they had you doing a great many things you didn't care all that much for. My goodness. Tell me what it is you can do. Rain told me she can make a computer dance. My sons, Jeffery and Tom, are very much into computers — well, anything electrical — and were amazed at what she could get from it so quickly. Tony is going to try and talk her into working with him on a few projects. If you'd not mind." Storm just looked at the other woman. "You're very protective of her. I didn't want to upset you when there was no need for it."

"Rain can and will do what she wants no matter what I tell her. Sometimes she does listen when our parents are around, especially. But as far as working with your son, that would be up to her. She digs into offshore accounts when she's bored and follows the trail back to see where the money came from. If it's gotten in some illegal way, she'll take it back. Mostly she just moves the money around when she finds it, never keeping much more than about ten percent for her to live on, but she's helped a great many people by giving them their money back. And when that isn't possible, she'll distribute it to places, like charities, that can certainly use it. However, as far as working with anyone, that would have to be between her and your son. By the way, I meant to thank you for taking her in. I do protect her from our parents when I can. They know she's what they call breakable. What they do to her is make her feel like the world is coming down on her, and she crumbles. They no longer try that on me."

"No. I would imagine not."

She rocked for a few minutes, and Storm reached for her sister. They could talk like this. Neither of them knew why or how, but she asked her if she was all right. And if she wanted to stay for dinner.

Yes, I'd like that. Very much so. I had some fun this afternoon working with Jeffery and Tony. They made me feel good about myself. I don't get that too often. Storm told her that she thought she was wonderful. *You don't count. You're supposed to be impressed with me. You're my sister.*

All right. We'll have dinner. I've spoken to Charlie, what he wants me to call him. He said he's going to have the place you were staying in torn down. He asked me if there was anything in the place you can't replace. I haven't any idea but told him I'd ask you. She said she didn't need anything but her clothing. *I'm thinking you need to leave that too if you don't mind. There are a lot of vermin in that place, and I don't just mean the bugs and rats. I wish I'd seen it sooner, Rain. I would have moved you into my place long before now.*

I've been meaning to get out for a while now too, but it was just too much. I'm glad now that I hadn't. Otherwise, our parents might well have found me. She could almost feel her sister's stress. *I'm coming down now. You'll be there?*

She told her where she was and sat down in one of the many other rockers on the deck. When two men came from the side of the house, it was all she could do not to pull out her gun and fire first and run second. They were flipping huge.

"These are two of my boys, Storm. The one on the step is Edwin. The other is Tony. They've been looking around the house for a couple of corn hole games we used to have." Storm told them where they were, not even giving it a thought as to why she'd done it. "You saw them? How? I had no idea you'd been here before."

"Tony saw them twice when he was looking in the small storage building." She turned and looked at Luna when she didn't say anything. "If they can see it, so can I. It's a nice little trick I have when I'm looking for something."

Edwin stared at her as he made his way to the rocker on the other side of her. Tony didn't move but did hold the door open for her sister when she came out of the house. Rain was making small talk while Edwin continued to stare at Storm.

Finally, she had enough and turned on him. "Did you drop a car on your head or something? I mean, you're big enough that you look as if you dead weight cars to keep in shape. Do I have dirt in my hair? Something in my teeth? What the hell is wrong with you?" He glanced at his mom, and Storm smacked him. "I asked you a question. I want an answer as to why you're looking at me like a fresh kill."

"I don't know a great deal about things that will happen to us as adults, but I think you're my mate. I'd be the first of us to have one. My brothers and I were born of a man to wolf and a wolf to woman. Everything we do is new to all of us." Storm leaned back in the rocker and thought about what he was saying. "My dad doesn't know either. I asked him. It was because my mom was introduced to him as his mate when she was still a full-blooded wolf. What are you thinking right now?"

"Nothing you want to know." She started rocking and made herself a little ill. When she stood up, so did Edwin. "If you crowd me, I'm going to hurt you where you stand. I'm sorry to be so brutal about this, but I have too much on my plate right now to have to deal with something new like this. I'll have to think."

"I would imagine you would. I do as well."

She started off the porch but turned to go into the house. She was both disappointed and happy that he didn't follow her. Storm cornered the first person she came to when she entered the living room.

"What's your name?" He told her. "All right, Garfield. I want you to go into the yard with me and spar with me. Not painfully, but just enough that I fall on my ass a couple of times and clear my head. Come on."

"Nope. Not going to happen." She asked him if he was afraid of her. "Yes, ma'am. Very much so. But more so of my big brother. If I so much as muss up your hair, he's going to take me apart limb by limb."

"That's stupid." He nodded and looked to her right. She did as well. Edwin was standing there saying nothing. "Would you really hurt him if he were to fight with me in the yard? When I asked him to?"

"No." She let out a long breath. "It would be just as he said, I'd kill him. Not that I'd want to. I love my family very much. But the need to protect you is very strong, and my wolf will do the killing."

Storm punched Edwin in the face, hard

enough that he fell back on his ass. When she told him to get up, he did so, then was back on his ass when she hit him again. Storm didn't know where all this violence was coming from, but she needed to feel something. Alive was the only thing she could think of. As he lay there, nursing his bloodied nose, she told him she needed to work off some pent-up anger.

"At me or someone else?" She said her parents. "That's all? You're not pissed at me for being stupid about killing my brother? You only need to boil off some anger?"

"Yes, and that doesn't mean you get to stand there while I do it, either. I want you to fight me. Not as hard as you would a man—clearly, you'd kill me if that were to happen. But I fucking need to have my noodle knocked around enough to be able to think a single thought without my head exploding into fifty more of them." He looked at his dad, then Edwin looked at her. "I'm betting that if I asked your mom to spar with me, she'd do it."

"I'm coming." Edwin stood up. He was much taller than her, by at least a foot, but she needed this to work off some of the anger so she could think. "But we do this outside. And if you want to stop, then you say so, and it's done.

Right?"

"Yes. But I don't want you to hold back too much. Some. I'd forgotten you were a wolf. But if you could do this for me, I'll be able to calm myself down." He nodded, and she followed him to the back of the house and into the yard. Before she was down the stairs, Edwin tripped her, and she landed on her face. "Great."

She had no idea how long they were at it, but she knew he was holding back a great deal. Secretly she was glad he had been. The way she was feeling right now, she was sure she'd be dead if he hadn't. Dropping to the ground on her knees, she put up her hand. She was finished.

Looking at Edwin, she was glad to see that he looked about as bad as she was feeling. They were both bloodied. She knew she was going to be sore tomorrow, too, if not tonight. Her knuckles were hurting, as well as her left ankle. Standing up, it was all she could do not to fall back down and just lay there. Making her way to the hose by the house, she rinsed off as much of the blood and grime as she could before handing the hose to him.

"Do you feel better?" She blew her nose straight into the grass and rinsed her face off with the cold water again. Telling Edwin that she did, Storm thanked him. He laughed. "When I first tripped you up, I thought for sure you were going to call it a day. But you gave as good as you got. I didn't know I needed that as well. Are you able to calmly talk about things now?"

"Not just yet." She looked up at him. "I've been holding that in for a while now. I had a bag I used, a punching bag, but it got busted the other day, and I've not had any time to replace it. I just needed it to make me feel better. It's not like I could just punch a man in the face too often without him pulling a weapon on me. It's violent, sure, but it takes my mind off of the shit going on up there long enough for me to get myself settled. Understand?"

"Not really, but I can understand needing to get out of your head. I usually read a good book or go on a run. Perhaps we can figure out a less bloody way for you to blow off some steam. I have the room in the house that I own—we own—that we could easily turn into a large gym that we can both use. And by the way, I don't lift cars unless I need to get it off someone." She turned off the water and turned to him. He was still a mess, but he was already healing. "What are you?"

"Just a person. I don't know. Do you see

something different?" All he did was nod. "Rain and I are sisters—not twins, but we both have this magic that surrounds us that we've never seen on anyone else. We can also communicate with each other from long distances. Like you would with your family. There are other things as well. The computer thing with Rain. I can, as you've seen, see things that others might have missed. It made me a good cop for a while."

"But not now, for some reason." She didn't even blink at him. "All right. That's good to know. You're healing. Could you do that before? I mean, this quickly?" Looking at her reflection in the window of the house, she could see that she was healing. Her lips weren't as swollen feeling, and she could see that her nose was no longer bleeding. Storm told him she hadn't been able to do that before. "That's a sure sign that you're my mate. Even though we've not exchanged anything, I can still share my magic with you so you can heal. Also, there is a good possibility that you're going to live for a very long time. I don't know that I would call it immortality, but I don't know what else it would be called."

She was given a shirt to put on that she was sure was Edwin's while her shirt and pants were being washed. While she was in the bathroom, Luna knocked on the door and asked if she'd been able to dress herself. Not sure what she meant, she opened the door to the beautiful woman.

"You should be able to think of things you'd like to wear, and it'll appear on you. Or not. I'm not sure. Charlie can do it. So can the boys and I. Edwin asked me to see if you were able to do it too." Instead of being dressed, her clothing appeared in her arms. "Well, that's close enough, don't you think? Good. If you don't mind, I'm going to toss out the other things. They're beyond repair anyway."

Getting dressed made her realize that every place on her body was in pain. Taking the two pain relievers that Rain had given her, Storm was sure it wasn't going to even put a dent in it. Going to the living room, she was happy to see that it was only Edwin and not his family. She was ready to talk to him now.

"I work for the government. They call it reconnaissance, but it's more like I have a connection to the person I'm looking for and can go right to him or her to bring them out to where they can be questioned or arrested. Rain can be and is helpful for me when I'm doing that sort of work. However, no one ever knows she's helping me. I'd like to keep her safe if I can." Edwin told her what he could do with phone calls. She sat down on the couch across from him as he told her what he'd gotten when he'd been on his way home. "Rain can take care of those for you. Even going so far as to figure out where they're being monitored. I'm assuming they're trying to pull you back in for some chair force job."

Edwin laughed. "Yes, recruiting of all things." She nodded. "There is more. What I can do, I mean. I have picked up one more thing so far that I didn't have before I met you. I can now trace people. Like your parents. I was simply thinking about them, and I knew they were staying at the bed and breakfast just outside of town and that your dad has on a girdle. Nothing that I really needed to know, but it was right there for me to see." Storm laughed, and he joined her. "You pick up anything other than getting clothing for yourself? I'd like to know it all, but I have a feeling we're going to be here all day if we start on that."

"Nothing yet other than the clothing thing. But then, I've not tried. I do have a question for you. What did you mean when you said you were all new to the man to wolf/wolf to human thing? I thought that was the way all shifters were." He

said his dad was changed when he was a man—
not changed by wolf ways, but by magic. Then
he told her about Romeo. "So this man follows
your dad around for days, then asks him to take
his job. As what, did he tell him?"

"Yes. The watcher of wolves." He didn't say
anything more, so she let her mind work through
that. Then when he did speak, she listened to
him intently. "My mom knew Dad was her mate
before Dad was changed. She took a walk with
him after he talked to Romeo. While he was
thinking about the information he'd gotten from
Romeo, hunters fired upon him. Dad said times
were difficult then, and they might well have
been just looking for meat. The shot nearly killed
him. Dad had sent Mom back to the compound
to warn the others, an act of unselfish kindness
that earned him a little more magic than Romeo
had given him. After the change, Dad was given
riches beyond simple money—lands that have
served us well, as well as a pack that is doing
much better than any other in the world."

"This money, it's what made you wealthy
then?" Edwin explained how the money from
the pack had never been theirs. The land had
been a great producer, and it had paved the way
for them. "Okay, so you made your money the

old-fashioned way by working hard and let the pack take what was meant for them to keep them safe. That's really awesome. Who was Romeo, and who gave your dad the extra magic that he got for being unselfish?"

Edwin smiled and stood up. When he came back after opening and closing the door to the deck out back, he handed her a small creature. When it stood up, she knew him to be a faerie. They stared at each other for what seemed an impossibly long time before he finally spoke.

"You're not human, my lady, but part wolf. I've not met your sister, but I believe she would be as well." She said her parents weren't wolves. "Nay, they'd not have to be. However, there must have been a pair or two of them along your bloodline back some time ago. My name is Chaplin. I've been working with the Griffin family for a great many years for my boss. Whatever questions you might have, I'd be the one to ask if the family cannot find one for you. Also, I know you to be magical too, but that is nothing to do with you being a wolf. Did you, by chance, have a traumatic birthing? The two of you?"

"I don't know. I mean, it never came up." She looked at Edwin when he sat down, then back at Chaplin. "Are you holding something back from me? I'll let you know right now. I don't care to have things given to me in bits and pieces. If you know something, I'd like to know what it is as well. I can't fix things when I have nothing to work with. Tell me what it is."

"All right. I have a way about me that lets me see things in people's heads. Your parents are going to kidnap your sister when they find her. They're not above killing you for the opportunity to get to your sister. They owe a great deal of money to the government for a scam that I don't understand. The agents, all sorts of them, they're looking for them as well. Also, Lord Edwin has his own troubles with the government. However, through no fault of his own." She asked him what else. "I can help your sister with your permission. She has a crippling disease that is keeping her from being safe. Should your family be able to find her, they'll use that against her. If she could be able to not just defend herself but get away too, she'll be all right."

"I can't give you permission for something that would be for my sister. If she allows you to help her, then I'll support her. But I won't talk her into anything if she's not all right with it." He smiled at her. "You've already figured out she'll let you."

"No, my lady. But you are very good to allow her to make this decision. And it will be a good one for not just her, but for you as well."

When Chaplin flew off, she sat there staring at the man across from her but not really seeing him. When he said her name, she looked into his beautiful brown eyes.

"How much more can you take tonight? The reason I ask is, I'm much too sore to go out to the yard and spar around anymore." After laughing with him, Storm told him she wasn't sure. "I do have some information on your parents. The government thing Chaplin doesn't understand is that they've never paid taxes. Not even when the two of you were children. Also, I'm not sure you know this or not, but you have a brother. His name is Georgie. He's been institutionalized since he was an infant."

"We found him a few years ago. He was in a shithole of a place before, but Rain and I paid for a better place for him so he'd get good care. Have you any idea what happened to him to put him there?" Edwin told her he was looking into it for her. "Thank you. I'm starving. I know that's rude, but I'm really hungry."

The dining room was empty of not just

people but food too. Almost as soon as the two
of them sat down, his family came in and sat as
well. Like a huge restaurant feeding an army,
food came from the kitchen in bowls and platters
that were hot and smelled like heaven, served by
so many people she wasn't sure how they didn't
trip over one another. She didn't know what was
going on, but she couldn't have been happier at
that moment. Even her sister joined them and
seemed to be enjoying the food and company as
well.

The family was polite at the table. No
shouting or bad manners. There was a great deal
of conversation, but it was calm. She had no idea
why, but she figured that being wolves, they'd
just leap on the table and have at it. Giggling a
little, she passed the mashed potatoes to her left
after putting a large mound of the fluffy veggies
on her own plate.

I've decided to get help from Chaplin. She
nodded at her sister, then smiled. *He explained
what would happen and how it would work. I would
very much like for you to be there with me.*

*Absolutely. I'll be right there by your side the
entire time.* She smiled back at her. *Edwin is my
mate. I have other things to tell you, but it can wait.
I'm glad you're going to be better, Rain. I think you'll*

enjoy it more than ever now that there is a family around that we can trust.

I do trust them, too, Storm. I don't know why, but I really do. She winked at her sister when she put an equally large pile of potatoes on her plate. *I'm going to work with Edwin's brothers too. I might be able to handle being around them if I feel better.*

After dinner, they were given rooms to stay in. Storm was much too full to walk back home, and she was nearly asleep when they started for their own rooms. Tomorrow she was going to confront her family and find out what the hell they thought they were doing. Whatever it was, they were going to regret coming around this time, even if she had to turn them in herself. She might well do that anyway.

Chapter 3

"There seems to be no end to the things that stupid people will do, George. Why are people hiding away our children? I couldn't get a single person to tell me where Rain might be. One of them looked up at the sky and said that rain wasn't forecasted until the end of the week. What the hell did that have to do with my daughter?" George just grunted. He'd been napping when she came down to the pool area earlier. Not that he didn't do that all the time — napping seemed to be his superpower. "George. Are you listening to me?"

"Yes. Rain is our daughter, Linda, but it's also a weather forecast statement. Why you wanted to name them after the weather the days they were born is beyond me. I'm just happy it wasn't snowing." She told him not to be ludicrous, that the girls had both been born in the summer. "I'm not being ludicrous. I'm making a — never mind. All we need to do is find Storm. She'll lead us right to her sister if for no other reason than the two of them are closer than we are. I've never seen anything like that, how close they are to each other. But then, I guess we weren't around them as much as they were together. While out, did you happen to notice any suits around?"

It took her a moment to realize he meant Feds and not a suit shop. Men and their names for things.

"No. But then, there isn't any way they could have found us already. Do you think?" George said he wasn't sure. "For that matter, I'm not either. They just seem to pop up when we least expect them. You don't think one of our daughters is telling them where we are, do you?"

"Doubtful. I mean, it's not been out yet that we're being hunted, do you think? I've been looking on the Internet, and there hasn't been a word about us on there." George laid his head back down on the lounger he was in. "This is a really nice place here. If I were able to, I'd stay here for months. I don't imagine it's all that special in the winter, do you?"

"I hate winter." Linda did too. And buggy summers. This place they were staying in had a nice pool and lovely fans that seemed to blow away any kind of nasty creatures that might bother her. Also, there were drinks in a large tub for them to drink when they wanted. It was only water, but it was better than having to go inside to get something out of their room. She looked around before speaking again. "How are we paying for this, George? I thought you said we used the last of our cash in gas money to get here."

"I found a wallet." Which meant he'd stolen one. "Not a lot of cards, which I was fine with, but a great deal of cash. I'm guessing it was payday or something. Good for us, but sad for the bastard that carried around that much cash on him all the time."

Money was never a big deal to them. If they had it, they would save some of it for emergencies. Also, they'd not go out and spend it stupidly, using it instead for buying food when they needed it. Gas money too. Even to give the girls a couple of dollars when they wanted something. Of course, they'd used the girls to get the money in the first place, so giving them money was like a payday for them. George had explained it to her as making them as guilty as they were about the money. But this trip was different than any other they'd been on before. They were hiding out until Rain helped them.

Storm would be a bigger payday for them. They both knew that. She had smarts that could get them in and out of places where the money was. They needed a big payoff about now, with everyone breathing down their necks. However, it was Rain that they could make do what they wanted. A little pressure would make her shut down. Or locking her in a closet worked too. Whatever it took to get her to do what they wanted.

But not Storm. Storm had learned early that what they were doing was hurting someone else. It didn't feel like that to Linda, but Storm refused to help at all unless they did something to Rain. That was their pressure point in getting her to do anything. Just hurt Rain, and Storm would crumble.

Then their children had started running off. Linda supposed that at their age, it could no longer be considered running off. But she really missed the days when she could simply make them come to her and do her bidding. Now the

IRS was after them about unpaid taxes. How the hell did they figure they owed them money when neither of them had worked a day in their lives?

She looked over at George. "You pay taxes on your income, right?" He eyed her with one eye closed. "We didn't work, George. How do we have to file taxes if we never had a W-12, or whatever it's called? We didn't file because we didn't work. And for them to come after us, that's just stupid. We don't owe them anything. Do we?"

"I haven't any idea how that works. I guess we could ask someone." He laid back down. "Look it up on the computer in the kitchen area. They said we could use it. Just go and figure it out, and perhaps we can get this settled before we run down the kids. And if you're right, we'll just keep the money for ourselves."

She did just that. The computer was something she'd never been any good at using. Looking things up wasn't the problem. It was how to word it so she could get just what she wanted. Sometimes she'd be tripped up on the spelling of things. Linda had always been a terrible speller. Once, she'd looked up potato recipes but had misspelled the word so badly it thought she was looking up prostitution for some reason. She'd gotten such a kick out of what had come up that she had decided she was going to call potatoes prostitutes from then on. However, that didn't work out as well as she'd thought. Restaurants didn't approve of their side dishes being referred to as women of the night.

Linda ended up with no more information than she had before sitting down. She had found a lovely dress she was going to see about purchasing when an ad popped up, but as far as the IRS, she was getting nothing. She decided to take a walk around town to see if there was one of those tax places around where she could ask questions.

The town was a lovely little place. She could understand why people would want to visit. However, there just wasn't enough going on all the time for her to be able to live there. There was a movie theater about half an hour away, she'd been told. A sad mall, also what she'd been told, and no real nightlife if you weren't into football or basketball. Frustrated that she wasn't having any luck in town either, she nearly went into one of the little shops when she saw her daughters.

Rain was a beautiful woman. A classic beauty, she'd been told. Long straight brown hair, brown eyes. She looked like she had never put on an ounce of weight since she'd started filling out as a woman. However, it was Storm that would draw attention to herself, and she'd never notice it.

Storm was a wild beauty. Her hair was dark and curly, almost blue-looking as it shone so well in the sunlight. Brown eyes too, but they were dark as well, like cocoa from a container. When she was upset, which by Linda's estimation was nearly all the time, her eyes would darken incredible more and show spots of blues and greens in them. Naming her Storm had been a perfect match. Right now, they were both coming toward her, laughing at something one of the three men behind them was saying.

"Mom. What are you doing slinking around? I thought for sure you'd be hiding out from the government. They are still looking for you." Linda told Storm she was working on that. "I'm sure you are. Why don't you just go home and work on it? Staying here will only piss me off, and that will make me have to hurt you."

"Do you hear the way she speaks to her mother?" None of the men even acknowledged her. "I'm Linda Hudson. These two ingrates are my daughters. And who might you be?"

She put out her hand, but no one seemed inclined to take it. When she asked them what was going on, one of the men put their arm over Storm's shoulder. It was a pure sign of possession, and she was completely surprised that Storm had allowed it. This wasn't like her at all.

"Not that you're going to get an opportunity to get to know him, but this is my fiancé, Edwin Griffin. The other two men are his brothers, Tony and Jeffery. Rain is going to be working with them." She asked, doing what. "Whatever they need her to do. And believe it or not, they don't want anything in return for it. What is it you're working out with the IRS?"

"Never mind that. Rain, I need you to come with me. I need a few things taken care of." She was walking back toward the little place they were staying when she realized that Rain had told her no and that she wasn't coming along like she should have done. "Rain. I said I need you to come with me."

"And I said no. I'm not going to do anything for either of you again. You are on your own for whatever scheme you have going on in your small mind." She looked at Storm before speaking to her again. "I've broken free of all the things you made me believe when I was a child. No one is going to take me apart if they figure out what I can do. Nor are they going to attach me to some kind of machine that will make it so they can read my thoughts. I'm happy. Working and on my way to being a much better person, no thanks to you. No. Whatever you want from me, I'm not going to give it to you. No matter what you do or say to me. I'm a grown woman, Mother, and I know you're the only one that has been hurting me, and I was letting you. But no more."

When they entered the little place beside them, Linda stood there for a full minute trying to wrap her head around the fact that Rain had gotten a backbone at some point. She didn't like it, no, but she did think it was funny. However, that didn't negate the fact that she was going to help her. Or Storm was. Either way, they were going to help out their parents, or else.

Turning to go to the store or building that her girls were in, Linda leapt back when one of the three men that had been with Storm was in front of her. He didn't move out of her way, either, but only blocked her again and again when she tried to go around him.

"What is your problem?" The man, she

thought he was Edward or something, said that she was his immediate problem. Then he corrected his name for her. "So? Edward. Edwin. Why is it you think I should care what you're called? You're harassing me, and I don't care for it."

"I don't care for you, so I guess on that venue we're even." She hadn't any idea what venue meant but let it go. "It means you and I are on the same wavelink. And yes, I am reading your mind. It's not all that difficult to do. It's so uncluttered with any sort of intelligence. As an answer to your question, no, you don't have to file a tax report if you have no income. However, I do believe you will have to show how you were able to live the lifestyle of having an endless supply of money. And I don't think you can actually own anything when you don't file. I'm assuming you still own your home, as well as the country home in California?" She told him she did before thinking that she shouldn't even be talking to him. "Did you pay the taxes on that? Or the home in another state? California does require you to pay real property taxes on it. As will anyone, I guess. Perhaps that, too, is why they want to speak to you. To figure out how you own two very substantial pieces of property, paying no taxes and having no income."

"How do you know all this? Are you a tax person?" Edwin told her that he read books. "That's it? You've read books. Well, goody for you. However, I still need to speak with my daughters. I'm their mother."

"Not a good one, however, are you, Linda? You never have been." She drew back her hand to slap the piss out of him. "I'm not human. And if your hand touches my face or any other part of my body, I will shift and kill you. I'm not the least bit squeamish about it either. I will tear you apart right here on this sidewalk. Go back to the place you're staying and leave my future wife and her sister alone."

Linda found herself alone on the street. The man was just going into the building not far from where she was, but the need to follow him to talk to Rain and Storm was gone. While she would eventually have to find the two of them, today wasn't going to be the day. The need to hide was riding her hard, but she made herself walk back to where the car was parked and get inside.

Her hands were shaking so badly that she had to sit there for several moments until she felt like she could drive without hurting herself. Even to start the car seemed like an impossibility right now. Breathing in and out, thinking, she didn't know what to do about the money now. Even if they didn't have income or had to file taxes, they had certainly lived up their lives. Mostly it was from their ability to make a buck into ten. Not a great deal of money, no, but it had been enough to live on. George had won the house in California in a card game. He had cheated, but since no one could prove it, it was theirs. Did they really have to pay taxes on houses that they owed nothing on?

"Instead of helping me, the questions are getting more and more complicated."

They'd had the income from Georgie until a few months ago. Then the home he was in figured out they were getting it and petitioned for the home to get it instead. They'd not been notified. Not that they could have done anything about it then, but it would have been nice to have had a few months more of it until…well, a few more years of it would be better than just cutting them off. She knew that much.

Driving back to the B&B, she thought about what to tell George. Everything, of course, but if she didn't have things lined up in the way of how it happened, he'd be bugging her about details and would make her have to start again and again. He was a stickler for details. It annoyed her, but she tried hard to make it easier on both of them.

She went right out to the pool area where he was still napping and told him everything that had happened, and in a good order too. Linda was very proud of herself until he started poking holes in what she'd said.

"What was the name of the building she went into? That could be helpful if we knew where she was working when we have to go get her. Is Storm still carrying a gun? I don't want to get my foot shot off because she gets a burr up her ass." She told him she'd not noticed. "How can you not notice something as important as the name of the place where Rain will be working, Linda? I've said this before to you. Details are what will be the difference between us getting out of something clean or not."

"It happened so quickly. I went into town to find one of those places that does taxes for people. You know which ones I mean, the places we see in the stores all the time." He said they were only out at tax time. "I don't even know when that is."

"April or before, I suppose." He laid back

down. "The next time you get it into your head to confront one of the girls, you let me know. I will want to record it for us to laugh at later. I'm betting they're having a good laugh about you standing there with your mouth hanging open wanting information, but too shell shocked to go get it."

There were times when she could gladly brain him. Like right now.

Getting up before she did something stupid, Linda made her way into the place. The woman was standing there at the sink when she came in. She asked to speak to her.

"Yes, of course. Why not." The woman started in on how she had guests coming in soon, and they'd have to move out. The rooms had been reserved for some time now. "But we're already here."

"Yes, but when I rented the room to your husband, he assured me you'd only be here for a couple of days. It's been five. I need the rooms. I'm sorry."

Sure she was. But instead of telling George, she went up to her room. Linda had a splitting headache.

~*~

Looking around his office, he wondered

why he'd never set one up before. It was nice to have his own things laid out in a nice order. His computer was locked all the time, but it only took him a second to get it open again. Also, he had his own printer, scanner, and a fax machine. The biggest bonus was that he didn't have to share his chair. He hated that more than he did sharing a desk.

"I have two questions to run by you." He smiled at Storm. "Am I interrupting something? You look sort of sappy. We're not going to have a problem with that, are we?"

"You don't like sappy? Or as I like to think of it, romantic?" She said she could handle romantic if he wasn't sappy too. "I guess I'll have to work on that since I haven't any idea what you're meaning. What is it you needed to ask me?"

"Yes. There is an issue with the White House computer system. I know what they're asking me. However, I don't understand why it's something they would need. They have a tracer on some things that are no longer reading." Edwin asked her if they told her who they were tracing. "I didn't ask, but then they wouldn't tell me anyway, would they? Anyway, they want me to come there and look into their system to see what the glitch is."

"Do they know you and I are mates?" She sat down in the unwrapped chair he'd gotten with his desk. "I'm getting to the reason. This tracer, did they happen to mention the last time they were able to track it?"

"Since leaving DC. Where are you going? You're making me think this tracer is on you." He didn't so much as blink at her. "I see. *When was the last time you had this room* debugged? Or do they even know where you live?"

"I don't know if it would be all that difficult to find me. I bought this house some time ago. And no, I've never thought about it being debugged. Can you do that?" She said she'd call Rain. *I might be able to do it, but I'd have to know the tone, I guess. How well is she able to find them?*

Quickly. And she can disarm them. But she'll tell you who is tracking you unless you already know that. Edwin told her. *I think we need to stop having conversations in this house and the others until we get this figured out. All right?*

He agreed. Edwin hadn't thought of his home having bugs, but he knew he should have. Storm went out of the house to make the call to her sister and came back in and sat across from him. Neither of them said a word until he had a thought.

You need to mark me so we can communicate with each other like I can with my sister. He agreed with her and asked her how. *Just make up something that has me coming to you to fix it. I don't know. You're the army guy.*

Edwin just caught himself from laughing out loud when he realized that he could pretend she was hurt in some way and could give her first aid.

"The wound on your arm." She frowned at him. "The other day, when you fell and cut your arm, I should have bandaged that up for you. I still can if you wish. I know it was a good cut and bled well, but I don't want it to get infected."

"Yes, of course. You never know what's going to get into a cut like this one." She came to him without any hesitation, and he bit down on her fingertip. As soon as it bled, he licked the wound closed, and she stood near him. "You have a first aid kit around here? The reason I'm asking is because my sister was burnt at the house too, and perhaps you can use some of your skills to wrap it up too."

As soon as Rain arrived, Storm spoke to her through their link. He was learning more and more about these two daily, and he was glad they were on his side. The thought of having them as enemies was frightening. They were beginning to think like someone he'd have arrested. Or killed. After nipping at Rain's finger, the two of them talked about the new office furniture as Rain walked around the room, pointing out not just bugs but what looked to him like a camera.

Some of the bugs are new. I'd say someone put them in over the last couple of days. The glue is still tacky. However, there are a great many of them that have been here for some time. He nodded, not even sure what he should think about this. Rain continued. *If you still have the shoes, I can look them over too. In fact, I'd love to have them and take them apart. I enjoy seeing how they put them together.*

You can have anything I have if you can help with this. She smiled at him, and it hit him how much Rain was like her sister. *Chaplin said you went through what he did for you nicely. How do you feel now?*

Free. He didn't ask anything more. Having a feeling that was exactly what she felt, he let it go. *Storm said you can back trace things. She can as well. Storm has had a great deal of practice with doing that if you'd rather not. Not that I don't think you can do it, but I want to give you that option.*

Her. She's very comfortable with the sort of

things she's been doing, don't you think? Rain smiled at him then. It was a delay, he realized, to not make him feel foolish by telling him something he could very well figure out for himself. *I'm retired army. Command sergeant major. Why would anyone want to keep track of my whereabouts?*

You've seen something that you shouldn't have? Storm can also help you with that. Again, she's good at seeing things you don't think you have. Also, it might be because you have some knowledge about one of them that they don't want you to spill. That one, I don't know. You'd have had to overhear or even to eavesdrop on a — what is it?

He stood there, then sat back down — twice, as a matter of fact. Edwin didn't know where to start or even if he could tell her at this moment. What he knew. The things he'd overheard and seen had never meant anything to him until just this minute.

I can't tell you like this. She nodded, telling him she understood. *It's worse than I thought. I mean, I didn't think about it until just now how I've been led down a rabbit hole, and I didn't even know it.*

We'll help you. Storm and I will protect you. Edwin didn't know why he thought his only way of coming out of it was for them to help him, but he knew it to be as true as he was sitting there. *Be calm, and have your brother bring the shoes here. I've turned off all the monitors as well as listening devices until we can get this fixed for you. Storm wants you to go out onto the deck and sit with your dad. He's here with another one of your brothers.*

Edwin didn't know how he made it out of the house. Suddenly he was sitting on the rocker with his head between his knees. Dad and Stone were talking about the weather, which he couldn't understand. He asked his dad.

"We're supposed to make small talk and not talk about how you're trying to kiss your own bottom." Edwin told his dad that under these circumstances, he could call it an ass. *Perhaps if I knew what you were upset about. It's all I can do to sit here and not have to go and find something to slay for you.*

I'm in deep shit here. Deeper than I ever imagined I'd be. Dad told him that Storm told him they'd take care of him. *Honestly, Dad, I'm thinking Storm and Rain might be the only people that can keep me out of federal prison. Not just because of who they are to us now, but because of the magic they both hold.*

Then we'll stay out of their way until they need us. You think they will? I'd like to help save you if I can. But if they're better at something, there isn't any reason at all why we'd want to butt in. Don't you agree? He said he did and looked down the driveway to see his mom driving up, as well as a couple of trucks he knew his brothers drove. "The troops. Rain or Storm must have called them in for some dinner. I'm a bit nervous if you want to know the truth, son. The things these two can do is scary. Not to mention, they seem to be stronger when they're working together. I'd feel sorry for their parents if I wasn't so blasted upset with them. Those two don't have a clue what they have in them girls, do they?"

"I don't think anyone does." Dad laughed, and he joined him. "Are we having dinner here? I think I'd love to have a nice thick steak with all the trimmings. I'll even go pick them up for us."

"Sounds like a good plan. Leave the girls here…no, that won't work. You take Storm if you can, and she might be able to shed some light on what is going on. If she does, then you let us know." Edwin told his dad that he would. "Son, I'm right proud of you. You didn't even think it was a bad idea to let your mate take over when you couldn't do something. It takes a big man to be able to admit that. And I bet that Storm will like it too."

"I love her." He was shocked that he really

did love Storm. Hugging his dad, he told him he'd be back. Then after hugging his mom and getting a list of things to pick up, Storm came out to see him. She looked worse than he felt. Something she'd found had upset her, and he wasn't sure he wanted to know. Getting into his car, he thought she'd need one here too when she told him she had one. "Great. After we get the fixings for dinner, we'll head by and pick it up. Does Rain have one too?"

"No, now that you mention it." She looked at him. He could see the worry on her face. "You're going to be just fine; you know that, don't you? I have fallen in love with you, Edwin. And the thought of anything happening to you scares me shitless."

"I love you too, love. And like you said, we'll get this taken care of, or you will, and we'll be just fine." He hoped so anyway. "Now tell me what you'd like for dessert. Mom said you should pick it out since we don't know your tastes as yet. There is a nice bakery on Main Street where we can pick up some things."

It was the hardest thing he'd done, talking about anything except what was really on his mind. She was better at the small talk thing than he was, so he left the talking to her. Almost as soon as they were home again, with both cars, Rain and Storm went out to the yard. He wasn't even worried about them getting hurt, but he did pity the person who tried to hurt them.

Smiling for the first time since this began, Edwin began to feel like he could come out on top with this. He wasn't sure how just yet, but he knew he'd be there, with the two most beautiful women he'd ever known at his side.

Chapter 4

She didn't go into the store with Edwin. Storm wasn't sure what kind of system the government might be tapped into, and right now, she didn't think it was a good idea for anyone to know they were together. After Edwin made his way into the store to get the steaks, Storm followed with her own cart to get some side things to go with them.

There were a great many bugs in his home. She thought perhaps she might well have preferred the creature kind and not the humans that were snooping where they didn't belong. The one thing that bothered her the most was that most of the house had been bugged long before he'd retired. Rain told her up to at least three or four years ago. What did he know?

They were going to talk tonight after everyone left. Rain was going to stay over so that she could get any questions she might have answered too. Storm's sister was a very different person since she'd had a long talk with Chaplin.

That had been all that was needed, he'd told her after Rain had taken a nap. To weed out some of the untruths their parents had told her about the magic, as well as a boost to her confidence. Even that, Chaplin said, was just a small tweak that made her feel good about the work she could be doing with the Griffin family, as well as someone believing in her that wasn't blood-related.

"You're telling me I didn't count by telling her she was amazing." He said it wasn't just that, but no, it didn't mean as much to her as a stranger saying it to her. "I guess I can understand that. It does feel good when someone acknowledges your work. In a not-my-sister sort of way."

Now here she was, waiting in line to pay for the potatoes, salad fixings, as well as corn on the cob to go with the steaks. She was just reaching for a bottle of cold water out of the fridge they had while waiting in line when Rain contacted her.

There is a man here looking for Edwin. He

said his name is Chad Wick. I think people should think carefully about fake names, or they just come off sounding really stupid. Anyway, he claims he has something that belongs to Edwin, and he needs to return it. Storm asked if she knew what it was. *No. He says it's for Edwin. Charlie is having a great time with the man, misunderstanding about everything he says. The man is much too funny to be released out on the public at any time. Anyway, I wanted to warn you that Chad Wick is here and that you should just wait at the car for the brothers to come and help you into the house and to carry the stuff in. Did you get macaroni salad like I asked?*

I did. She looked at the large tub of the nasty stuff her sister seemed to love over everything else edible in the world. *Do you think he's there because he's figured out that the cameras and microphones have been disabled? Or do you think he really has something that belongs to Edwin? Who I've fallen in love with, by the way.*

Duh. Anyone can see that you love each other. I don't know about the man. However, he is really jumpy, like he's afraid something is going to come out of the house and have him for dinner. I'm thinking he knows the people here are wolves, and whatever he's doing is a no-no, and he's afraid. Storm said she liked that theory. *As do I. I've been looking around the yard too. There are cameras installed outside the house, but Jeffery did those. I've been working on them, and I do believe I've made them so they can't be hacked into. I wouldn't put anything past these people to just horn right in on someone else's hard work putting them up.*

Storm put the last of her things on the belt and glanced at Edwin as he made his way to the car they'd parked around back. Asking her sister if she was able to do the same to the cameras all over town, Rain said she could do that too and that she'd take care of them. Storm asked her how she knew how to do that.

I've no idea. But the more I hang around this family, the more I'm finding out I can do. Like playing around with the cameras I found in the living room. I made it, so they were only getting the feed from a commercial station. That's all. And at the highest volume. She laughed with Rain as she paid for the things she'd gotten. *I'll see you when you get here. Remember, Storm, wait in the car for the guys to come out and get you. There is no point in showing our hand right away.*

She and Edwin talked about nothing much in the car. Telling him about Chad Wick—her sister was right; it was a stupid name—he said he had no idea who it would be and left it at that.

Storm also told him about her going in the back way with his brothers surrounding her.

In no time at all, they were at the house. She did just as she'd been instructed and waited for Stone and Harman to come out to get her. They didn't talk about anything but the food, but she could tell they were nervous for their big brother. She was too.

~*~

"May I help you?" Chad turned around and smiled. Rain had been right when she warned him that the man was nervous. Edwin didn't take the hand that was offered, nor did he acknowledge it in any way. "My father said you have something for me. I don't know what it would be. I know I have all the things I left there with."

"Here you go." Just looking at it, Edwin knew what it was but didn't take it. Instead, he told the man it wasn't his. "Sure it is. It was in your desk when you left. I thought I'd just bring it out here to you and hope for a nice dinner for doing it."

The smile might have been nice had it reached his eyes. Edwin told him again that the thing, whatever it was, wasn't his. Chad was nodding even before he finished telling him that for the second time.

"It's a portable phone charger. This one is a nice one too. I bet it works really well." Edwin told him he wouldn't know. "It's yours, Edwin. I know it is. I've seen you use it around the offices."

"I don't know how that is possible, as I don't own a cell phone, much less a portable charger for one." Chad looked at him like he was trying to judge if he was joking or not. "It's not mine. As I said to you several times now. You can take it back and put it in lost and found like you should have in the first place. That thing isn't mine."

"Surely you have a phone." Edwin simply shook his head. "Christ, how do you communicate with your family if you're not using one? Or, for that matter, take a shit without a phone. I use mine for everything from making a grocery list to reminding me to send flowers to my mom on Mother's Day."

"I don't need a phone to remind me that my mom's special day is coming up. I write it down on a piece of paper if it's more than a few things to be picked up when I'm shopping. As for taking a crap? I don't understand the correlation between the phone and a bathroom break, but it doesn't matter. That thing doesn't belong to me.

Take it back with you." Chad told him he had to take it. "I *have* to take it? Why is that?"

"What I mean is, I can't take it back. I've already signed it out that I was bringing it to you. Can't you put it in your house, and maybe someday you'll come around to this century and get yourself a phone?" Edwin asked him if he was being a smart ass. "No, sir. I'm sorry if it sounded that way, but I've driven all the way out here to bring you this, and now you don't want it back."

"I don't want it back, as you put it, because it was never mine in the first place. Why aren't you understanding that? The charger isn't mine because I don't own, nor have I ever owned, a cell phone." Edwin crossed his arms over his chest. He knew he was intimidating standing like this, but right now, he wanted to be just that. "Look. I don't know you from anyone, and you're starting to get on my nerves. I want you to get into your car and get off my property. Your insistence about the phone charger is a little creepy."

"Look, I'll just leave it here." Chad walked up to the railing around the deck and put the charger gently, too gently, on the rail. When it was steady, he walked back to where he'd been standing before. "There. Now you can do with it whatever you wish. Take it in the house, shove it in a drawer. Whatever. It's yours. I would like to use your bathroom before I leave. And perhaps have a quick look around. This is a wonderful home."

"Thank you. I love it too. This charger, it's mine, you said." Chad seemed satisfied that he'd done his duty or whatever he'd been sent out here for. "And as you said, I can do whatever I want with it."

"Yes. Take it inside, shove it away until you need it." Edwin picked it up, and he heard the man's audible sigh of relief. But it was short-lived. Dropping it on the sidewalk, Edwin crushed it with the help of his wolf and his boot until it was nothing more than broken plastic. "What the hell did you do that for? You should have just taken it in the house."

"You said it was mine and that I could do whatever I wanted. I did that. Now you don't have to worry over it anymore, and I won't be out trying to satisfy some kind of inner need you have for me to have a cell phone simply so I can use it. It's gone." The anger on Chad's face was there. He wasn't even trying to mask it. "It was just a charger, as you said. Now it's gone, and you can be on your way back to—"

"You have no idea what you've done." Edwin looked down at the mess on the sidewalk, then back at Chad. "All you had to do was put it in the house, and that would be it. Now you've smashed it, and it won't work at all now."

"For what purpose did he need it in his house?" Rain came out on the deck then. She looked like a beautiful specter. "You brought that thing here for a purpose. You'll tell me what it was right now."

"They said all the cameras and mics were down. That once that device was in the house, it would be able to reset them, so they were up and running again." The man looked like he was in a trance. He spoke in a monotone voice that sounded like something from an old movie. Rain asked him who had sent him. "Mr. Jeckle and Mr. Hyde. I don't think those are their real names, but I didn't care because they paid me five grand to come out here and make sure it got into the house. Now it's busted to fuck."

"What else were you to do when you got here?" The man fought against the magic, and it was making his nose bleed. "This will go a good deal better on you if you were to just answer the questions. What else was your job?"

"To make sure the house hadn't been

messed with. Like the cameras and other devices that had been put in. I have a few hundred illegal drugs, too, that I was to put into one of the bathrooms before I leave so Edwin would be caught with them. It was a way for them to get him out of the house for a few days so someone could come in and figure out what was going on with their setup." Chad looked at Rain then. "They told me that if I didn't get him to take the device, I was to be killed when I returned. Now I'm going to die because he just couldn't do what I wanted and take the fucking thing."

"You're going to die, you moron, because you knew that doing this wasn't the right thing to do. Also, because you didn't do your homework on the man you were working to get put in jail. You dying will save me a lot of time trying to make sure you're not up to no good. Give me the phone number to the place you were to call when you returned." He spouted off the numbers quickly. Rain had him do it once more so she could make sure he got it right. "When you leave here, you go straight to the place you were to meet the men and tell them just what happened today. Understand me?"

"They're going to kill me."

Rain said nothing but did look at Edwin as

if to ask if he cared that the man might lose his life over this. After shrugging, Edwin sat down on the step as he listened to Rain telling Chad what he was to do once he told them what had happened.

"His name really is Chad Wick." Edwin asked Storm what else she knew about him. "He's a criminal of the worst sort. He's into drugs, women, and murder. Someone got him out of prison just so he could come here. I have a feeling that once he was finished with you, he was going to be dead anyway. And whoever sent him is going to say he was an escaped prisoner."

"Can you figure out what the device was for? I mean, like was it really to reset the devices in our house?" She said in theory it was, but with Rain working on them, it was doubtful it would have worked. "I think she's getting stronger with every breath she takes. I'm afraid of her if you want to know the truth. You as well. You weren't this strong before, were you?"

"Not even close. Rain could do some of the things she has done here, but not everything. I can not only see what this guy has seen with my magic, but it's like I have this video recorder in my mind that lets me see the event as it happens. From different angles too." Edwin asked her if she could see who Chad had spoken to. "No, sadly, he never spoke directly to them except via the phone. His release paperwork wasn't signed, so there is no tracing that back either. I'm thinking this isn't the first time that whoever is in charge of this thing has used prisoners. They were too slick at it. Everything worked out quickly too. For him to be here at this time means they had him in a holding pattern just waiting for something to happen."

"I was thinking the same thing. It looks like the guy is leaving. He's still bitching about the fact he's going to be killed." She told him what she knew about his sentencing. "So they just got a lifer out to come here and hand me a device. I wonder if he's left a trail of bodies on his way here. That would be murder tacked onto the person in charge of this."

"Are you going to tell me what it is you saw?" Edwin looked at the dust as it flew up behind the car leaving. "I could look, but since I'm not sure what it is that has you so spooked, I'd only be looking and not helping you."

"Can we do this later? I'd really like to have a good family dinner with you guys. After they leave, I'll sit you and Rain down and tell you everything I know." She said she had some things to tell him about her parents as well. "Just one more thing to put on our to-do list, I think. Besides, I think my dad wants to just go there and drag them into the woods and see how they fare with the pack after them. That might just be too funny not to have him at least try, don't you think?"

When he headed into the house, Edwin stopped to see if Rain was all right. When she smiled and nodded, he nearly walked away when she suddenly broke down into tears. Holding her while she sobbed about how she had sent that man to his death, he wasn't sure what he should tell her or how. When she looked up at him, they both smiled.

"I know he's a bad man. He was in prison for murdering ten people that laughed when he walked into a room. It's doubtful they even noticed him, but he pulled out a gun and killed them all. Not only adults but children as well." He asked her what had her so upset then. "I'm going to be responsible for his actual death. I've never thought of that before."

"The moment he pulled out that gun and pointed it toward those people in the room with him was the day he was responsible for his own death. By doing what you've done here today, you're going to see that justice is served. Did you pull the trigger either time? No, you didn't. Because of your help, the man will be pulled off the streets and into hell, where he belongs." Rain told him she could get used to having a big brother around once in a while. "You have five more of them. Also, parents, if you're inclined to think of them like that. We've all taken you and Storm into our hearts, and we love you like you're our own sister. Ask any of them. I'm betting they'll do just about anything you want for what you did here today."

"I'm afraid of myself. I can do shit I never thought of before. And now, that's all I have to do, think of it, and I can do it. What the hell am I? Or Storm, for that matter. We're not your average shifter wolves, I don't think." He told her he didn't think so either. "I was hoping you'd tell me I was wrong. That we're just plain shifters too."

"I won't lie to you. You and Storm scare me a little as well. However, and I hope this is true, neither of you will harm me so long as I don't harm you. Right?" She kissed him on the cheek as she walked away. "Right? Am I right, Rain?"

Now he was more frightened than before.

Shaking his head, he headed to the kitchen to see what he could help with. The macaroni salad was in a huge bowl, and Edwin couldn't help himself but found a spoon and took a large taste of it. His moan had him realizing that everyone was staring at him.

"No one likes this here, so I get it where I can." They still stared at him. "What did I do wrong now?"

"That's Rain's favorite." He looked at the woman across from him as his mom continued. "She was so happy she had a lot and wouldn't have to share. Now here you go and take about half of it on a single bite. I raised you to be more polite than that, son."

"I'm so sorry." When everyone, including Rain, laughed, he did as well. Still nervous, he told her again he was sorry. "The only time I get this is when I buy a container for myself. The little ones are too small for me to enjoy it, and the large ones, like I'm assuming this one came in, are simply too much, and I make myself a little ill trying to finish it. From now on, when you want some, just get two containers, and you and I will make a meal out of it. All by ourselves."

"Deal."

They all sat down a few minutes later to a

very delicious meal. Between the two of them, he and Rain finished off all the salad, and it was just enough for them. After dinner, instead of going to the living room, as they normally did, they sat around the table and talked about anything and everything. Then Storm's parents were brought up. When his mom started laughing, they begged her to tell them what was so funny.

"You all know Margie. She's the owner of the pretty little place the Hudsons are staying at. Anyway, she's been telling them for the last few days that they had to move out, as she has people coming in and the place will be filled up. When that didn't work, she called me. You see, she didn't want to hurt Storm or Rain's feelings if she had to call the police." Storm asked her if she told her they'd not care. "I did. So when they said that since they were there—that mother of yours is a nasty sort of person, isn't she?—well, they were all set to stay. Since they'd been hanging out at the pool most days, she and I went into their room, packed them all up with the help of the police, and set their things out on the front sidewalk."

Mom started laughing again, and it made them laugh as well. Storm asked if she'd gotten them out, and at that point, all Mom could do was laugh harder. When she finally calmed down a bit, she finished up the story.

"Margie is a member of our pack, as you know. While not wolf, her mate is. She called Alex up and told him she needed some of the men to come by and scare off some squatters. As soon as they showed up, we both knew it was going to be a great deal of fun." Mom was laughing again and tried twice more to tell them the rest before she could. "You should have seen them trying to get out of the pool and out of the backyard. Margie had locked the outside doors by then, and they went to every single door, pulling on them to try and get away. There was Alex and the others, biting them on the butts and snapping at their heels. I don't think I've enjoyed anything having to get humans their comeuppance as much as I did that. Goodness. The best part. Their things out front had been picked up by the trash company, as we both never even thought of it being trash day. They're not only homeless right now, but they're in bathing suits with nary a towel between them. Not only that, but your father is bleeding badly — not life threatening at all, but to hear him talk about it, he's moments from death. Your mom is a little worse for wear in that she's got herself a sprained ankle. Oh my, honey, I wish I had remembered to call you over to see it going on. It was a sight to see. I do hope you're not upset with us."

"Not at all." Storm looked at him. "I love you, Edwin Griffin, and I think I've found the family I've always been wanting. Right here."

"Why, thank you, Storm."

Rain said the same thing to the family that she was happy to have them in her corner, and it made him feel like he'd been given the best gifts in his life. A mate and a sister all in one swoop.

After the table was cleaned up, they did end up on the back deck. He was glad now that he'd thought to purchase extra seats to have back here and have the deck enlarged to accommodate them all. As the night began to creep into the evening sunset, he was still there when his parents and family left, leaving the three of them to talk about the events of the day.

"I've been able to backtrack on the calls Chad made. They were made from a burner phone from inside the White House." He asked Storm if she knew who had made them. "Not yet. I'm working on it. Mike, the president, has his own computer that he keeps under the bed. I don't know how secure he thinks that is, but that's where he hides it. His wife, while not doing anything about the trouble you're going to face, is well aware of it. Even offering up suggestions on how to make you pay. That part I'm a little fuzzy on. Did you shit in her oats or something?"

"Sort of. When she was hosting a dinner when I was there, she wasn't following protocol, and I told her. It was a huge mistake that may have cost relationships overseas. I stepped in just in time to stop her and to embarrass her at the same time. She's never forgiven me. What else have you found out? Do you know why they're after me? I can tell you what it is I've seen if that helps."

"I know." Rain looked at him, then her sister. "You tell him. I think he already has a good idea about why he's being tagged to be the fall guy, but it would be good to get it out there, so we have all the details."

"Six months ago, you were called to the White House on another matter. Do you remember what it was?" He told her he was supposed to have a food taster come in at the request of the diplomat coming in. "Yes, and you saw something that had you making the staff trash all the tainted food before anyone arrived."

"A staffer for the president was taking spoonfuls of rat poison and putting it on each of the dishes after the taster tested them. She claimed she thought it was paprika, but I don't think anyone ever followed up on it, as she killed herself the next day." He looked at Storm. "They murdered her too, didn't they? And I'm the only witness to the crime, so I must go as well."

"Something along those lines. It wasn't just the poison you caught onto either. You also saw that the wine bottles were being tampered with." He thought about it and realized she was right. "There were special dots put on the one for the president and his family, as well as the vice president, so they'd know which ones to drink from. You didn't do anything about it at the time, but since you'd caught the food poisoning and had it all dumped out, the staff also got rid of the wine."

"Why now? After, like you said, six months, why are they trying to make me the fall guy for this? And with me being out of the service?" He watched them both. Then it hit him what he'd missed in all this. "It's an election year. They're going to pin this on me, an honorably decorated retired major, to show the world they're up on things better than anyone had ever been before."

"Yes." There was more, and he asked them for it all. "When you fall, you're going to take your family with you. The wealthy Griffins are going to be said to have robbed, stolen, and cheated their way to their money. Not only that, but they have plans to expose you for being a shifter. They don't know what you are, mind you, but they figure that by pissing you off enough, you'll let your true colors come out, and they'll be right. They'll both look like the mighty conquerers, and you and your family will look like frauds. Worse than that, you'll be put in military prison for the rest of your life, and that will be the end of it. The way they reason it, anyway."

"Anything else?" She said she'd been hired to get with him and try to strike up a relationship with him to get all the intel she could. That actually made him laugh. "I had hoped you'd see it that way, Mr. Griffin. I'm planning on sticking to you like glue. And keeping you safe while I'm at it. Rain and I have a plan, but in order for it to work, we're going to need you to take care of our parents. Neither one of us wants to be distracted with dealing with them and this with the country."

"This is a royal fuck up, isn't it?" Rain told him it wasn't going to be. They had the upper hand in this. "I hope so. I don't want to be responsible for killing the fucking bastards when I just found my mate. And the best sister that a man could ask for."

"Thank you for that. If you can run point on Mom and Dad, I assure you that if you do what we tell you as well as your parents, you'll be just fine. In fact, more than likely better than fine." Edwin told them both that he'd take care of their parents. "Good. Then we're going to work on the rest. Just be careful. This stuff we can both do is new to us, and we don't want to hurt any of you with it. It would be great if you were to tell your family we'll need their full cooperation, and only then can we get started. The first thing we need to do is to get into the computers at the White House. I'm going to work on that now."

Rain got up and left them sitting here.

"Do I want to know?" Storm told him he more than likely didn't. "Are my brothers helping with this part?"

"Yes. That's all you need to know for now." He agreed with her. "Edwin, no one is going to hurt your family. My family. I promise you that Rain and I will fix this, and heads will roll."

"So long as it's not mine or the rest of the family's, I'll be happy too." She told him they'd be just fine. "Yes, so you keep telling me. I still worry. For as much as you tell me not to worry, you have this, I do worry about you and Rain. I want you to be safe as well."

"Oh, trust me. No one will have any idea what the hell happened when it does. The world will think you and yours are the best there is. Since I already know that, I'm going to let them think that as well. From a distance."

She was laughing when she entered the house. Edwin sat there for several more minutes before he laughed and entered the house as well.

Whatever was going to happen, he'd be ready for it. He wouldn't get involved with it either unless they asked. They were good at this, even being new at their magic, and he was glad once again that they were on his side.

Chapter 5

Mike put the phone back in the cradle and looked at Jamison, who was sitting across from him. For the past three days, he'd been trying to get in touch with Edwin, to no avail. The phone number he had for the man was disconnected, and there really wasn't a cell phone in the man's name, ever. How was it even possible that no one had noticed that before now?

"I take it you've not been able to get in touch with him." Mike told Jamison he'd been trying. "I have as well. Then today the phone number is no longer a working one. How much do you think that idiot Wick told them before he came back here telling us that people knew where he was?"

"Since he knew very little, I don't think

anything that is going to bite us in the ass. Did I tell you that his body was found? Just like we planned. An escaped prisoner caught just outside the prison. Christ, there aren't even any good criminals around when you need them." They both laughed a little, but they were pissed because things were not going their way. Mike thought about the first attempt to get Edwin out of their way. "When he figured out about the poison that day, I thought for sure he'd figure out who had ordered it. It was the only reason I had him find a taster for the sheik that was coming in, so he'd be in the kitchen to be blamed for the mess. Who would have ever thought he'd be that ballsy and have all the shit thrown out? Christ, that was a fucking mess."

"All night, I drank bottled water for fear that the bottles of wine hadn't been marked. And he'd had it tossed out as well. Even Emma was pissy about having to drink water. She'd wanted to have some very expensive wine too." Jamison leaned back in his chair before continuing. "We're going to have to step up our game on this, Mike. The election platform is starting to gear up, and I really like where I am in the grand scheme of things. I know you do as well."

"I do. Emma told me if she had to move

out before she got to have the entire place redecorated, she was going to leave me. Like I need one more bit of pressure put on me right now." Jamison said his wife was doing the same thing. She wanted to travel more as the lady vice president. "I have to tell you, Jamison, we couldn't have picked two better people to be our wives. They're as devious as we are about shit. When my wife had it all figured out about how to make it look like your secretary had killed herself after the debacle in the kitchen that night, I thought I'd better be staying on her good side from now on. No one questioned at all about whether or not she'd actually done it. I have to admit, I'm a little afraid of her. There is no telling what Emma would do to get me out of the picture if I were to mess up."

The room they were in was always checked for bugs. There wasn't any way that anyone could get into this room without his permission, but it didn't stop him from checking every single day. However, he had his own bugs in place, a camera too. There was no way he was going to be caught holding his own balls if this shit ever came out. Of course, he spent most of the night after every meeting in this room going over the recordings to take out what he'd said. He wasn't stupid enough to think they'd believe him if he said he was leading Jamison on into telling the truth.

There was no topic they didn't discuss either, from the amount of money they'd been able to put away to the things they were going to do with another term in the White House together. So far, they were worth billions, each of them putting money into two separate accounts in the event that one of them got into trouble. The other would help take care of their families. Mike had no such plans to do anything with Ellen. He couldn't stand to be around her enough to figure out what she might need when Jamison was caught. And he would be, too. Right along with Griffin.

He hated that man, with every fiber of his being. And it wasn't just the dinner he'd fucked up for him, but the amount of money he'd lost when the sheik had heard about the trouble they'd had in the kitchen. Had he been there when it went down, Mike wouldn't have allowed Griffin anywhere near the man. But as it turned out, he went directly to him and told him what he'd found. The man had left without a word about a war starting up between their two countries over the attempt on his life. Nor how the gas prices were going to be over the top because of it. He had believed Edwin when he told him he thought it to be a mistake.

It had been so well taken care of that not a ripple of it went out to the news reports, nor was there even a conspiracy element on the Internet about it, the place he'd been feeding shit to before he'd been elected president almost three years ago now.

"That woman, Rising Star. Have you heard from her since telling her to take care that she snuggles up to Griffin?" He pulled the email from his desk and handed it to Jamison. "So she'll do it. Good. And when this is done, we'll have to figure out a way to keep her name out of the paper. If we have it. Do you know who she really is?"

"No. I thought I could go down the list of retirees this month and find a woman that could be her. But there were fifty women retiring in the last six weeks, and not one of them had a name that would make me think that Rising Star was her. The file we have for her has no picture. No prints on the uncompleted paperwork, nor is there a single person that seems to understand how that happened. I don't even have a print of her pay stubs, as it was arranged before I came into office that her money was to be sent to an account with no address on it. Within fifteen minutes of the money being in the account, it's gone. No IP address to follow. The trail begins and ends right there. Whoever this person is, and I'm beginning to think it's a man, they certainly know their shit about moving money around. If I could find them, I'd have them move ours around for us." Jamison thought that would have been a great idea. "As it is now, I have an email address that is so well protected that the people on our end of the computers haven't any idea where the emails come from either. Or, for that matter, how they're opened. They're supposed to be notified when the person opens the email, but we get nothing back unless Rising Star answers us. I suppose in what she does for us, it would be very important that no one knows who she is. But Christ, everyone is so secretive nowadays. They don't even trust their president with information."

"I wish I could help you there, Mike, but I am worse at computers than anyone around. Even my grandkids are better at them than I will ever be. Don't even get me started on programming a remote or changing the television from one media to the next. I can barely get it turned down without much in the way of help." Mike thought of himself as an expert, but this Rising Star person was much better. He'd been trying to catch her for months with no success. "I don't want to raise any red flags about this, but do we have anyone on the hook that has a great deal of computer wizardry?"

"Not that I want to take the chance in figuring out if they can be trusted." He looked at the clock on the wall behind him. "I have an appointment in an hour with the IRS. There is a couple claiming that they shouldn't have to pay taxes because they don't have a job. Normally I'd not have a thing to do with this sort of crap, but they live in the town where Griffin and his family live. They own some houses or some other shit. I've downloaded a new game on my computer so I can keep my head out of it while they work with them. That is a department I do not fuck with."

"Yeah, me either. They can rip you apart and make you broke before you get in the door."

It wasn't that bad, but he understood where Jamison was coming from. His own parents had lost everything a decade or so ago when they decided to take on the Internal Revenue Service. He was still bitter about it.

When Jamison left him, Mike took all the recordings and put them in the safe. He'd been changing out the passcode on the safe every week like clockwork since he'd had it brought into this room. It was a requirement of the program on the safe to do that. Now all he did was change the last number to the next. The numbers were 4579. Tomorrow, the end of the week, it would be 4780. It was fucking easy to forget, and he didn't have time to write it down every time he changed it.

Looking into the safe, he realized he was going to have to make another drop to the boat offshore that he owned. The sucker, even for as big as it was, had too much stuff in it now. Closing up, he picked up the phone to talk to his wife. She was starting to get on his nerves about stuff too much of late as well.

"Did you make plans to go to a meeting this evening with Agent Jepson about some kind of tax evasion?" He told her what was going on. "So you did forget that we had a dinner gala at the church. Mike, I'm not going to go there alone. It's embarrassing to not have you around when I have these things. I told you the last time you skipped out on me that I won't do it again. The very least you can do is come with me. This is a charity event for the new library wing at the hospital."

"I did forget. Christ. I need one of those little calendars I can carry around with me all the time." She told him he had one. It was called a cell phone. "I forgot, all right. I'll call Jepson now and tell him something has come up. You know, I have plans too on occasion." She simply hung up on him. Yes, he thought, he could really begin to hate her.

Jepson was understanding, of course. After all, he told him, Mike was running an entire nation. He was, but with a great deal of help from a lot of people. Sitting down at his desk in the big office, as he'd been calling it for years now, he made busy work until it was time to go up and get dressed for this gala event.

Emma wasn't speaking to him, which thrilled him to no end. He knew when they got to the church she'd be all lovely dovey with him and put up the picture of the perfect couple. She'd campaign for him, do a little hand shaking in his honor, and all he had to do in return was to keep his mouth shut on what a fucking cunt she was, and then later, turn his head when she wanted to have an affair.

They would, at times, be fighting for the

same woman. Mike had known his wife was a hitter for the other team, so to speak when he proposed to her. But she was beautiful, built, and had a great many ancestors in her background that made him look like the blue blood he'd always wanted to be. Mike didn't know why he didn't think of it earlier about killing her off and reaping the votes from that. But frankly, she was just too smart for him to get out of a relationship with her. So, this plan with Griffin had come up.

The man was stinking rich too, had a great-looking body and a face that made women and a few hundred men swoon. A baby face that made you think that no matter how much older he got, he would still look this good. Another reason to hate the man. He was also a good man — very few of them left, he thought. Kind to people. And a family man. The fucking bastard would head home rather than hang out at the White House with him.

Then he'd seen too much. It had been Mike's plan to use the sympathy vote when he was elected president the first time. He had planned to ride that horse like it was his bitch, and he was a bronco rider. However, finding a person, anyone, that would make the country mourn their passing had been nearly impossible.

He was sure there were a few good people in DC. However, finding them and using them had been a different matter altogether.

As they were getting out of the limo, Emma turned to him. "I've been thinking about this man, Griffin." She fixed his tie for him as she barely moved her lips to talk to him. "There could be a horrific accident on his way here for a nice dinner to get to meet the family that brought this paragon of manliness into the world. It would play well to have them all killed off." Then she turned and walked into the church just ahead of the secret service.

It had merit, he thought. Very wealthy people coming for an honor dinner for a highly decorated officer? One who had fought in a couple of overseas wars? Mike had very little information on the man's personal life. He did know he had parents but knew very little about them other than they were wealthy too. Edwin was forever visiting them, wasn't he? Or so he'd said all those times he went off site.

The more he thought about it, the better he liked it. As he mingled around the room, making the right nods when necessary, shaking hands with whoever was close enough to take his, Mike did nothing but plan and plan what he wanted to do.

Just as he was starting to see the way it could go down, he saw someone from across the room that he thought he wanted to get to know, in a biblical way. Mike made his way toward the open doors that led out to the cemetery and saw the woman standing next to the headstone of some old priest or something. Going up to her, he smiled as he said hello. When she turned, he felt not just his cock get hard for the beauty staring at him, but his entire body was ready to throw her to the ground and take her right there among the dead.

"Don't get ahead of yourself, dumbass. I'm not here for a fuck with you. I'm here to talk." He told her who he was. "Don't you think I'd know that before I said I was here to talk to you? Christ, and they trust you with the country. My name is Rising Star."

~*~

Storm watched his face as it sank in as to who she was. He wasn't any better looking close up than he was on the television with all the filters and make up they put on him. Waiting for him to get a fucking clue, she told her sister what was going on.

I can get into the safe now too. The wolf that is

helping wants to be a part of Charlie's pack when this is over. Provided he doesn't get killed. He's about as antsy as I ever was when our parents came around. All right. I'm getting it opened up now. Mike was going on about having her put up in an apartment when she put up her hand. *Keep him there just a little while longer, and the safe will be empty.*

Telling Rain she would, Storm leaned against the headstone that was bugged and had two cameras pointing right at the idiot. This was just the starting point of getting the prick out of the way.

"I'm not going to fuck you. Or anything else, for that matter. I'm here to find out what you want from Griffin." He asked her what she'd been told. "I'll ask the questions. You're going to answer them. What is it you hope to gain by all this shit you're having me do to him?"

"Intel. If nothing else, we're going to establish a way to get him out of the way. He's bad news—you knew that, didn't you? I mean, you were told that." She said all she'd been told was that she was to fuck him. "Yes, lucky man. After this is over, and I'm in the White House again, we'll have to arrange an all-nighter, just the two of us."

"Fucking between the two of us isn't going

to happen. Not in any way, shape, or form. Answer the questions. Why are you targeting a man that seems to be a great deal nicer than you are? Which, when you think about it, isn't all that difficult." Waller told her she wounded him. "I only wish that were true. I'd dig a hole right here and bury you alive. Griffin, from what I've been able to tell, is nothing but a good guy. There are no skeletons in his closet. He has a big family that he seems to love and a wife that he worships. Which means I'm not going to be able to cozy up to him as you wanted."

"Damn, but that really sucks. All right, we'll hit up on plan two. I'm going to have them come here, all of them, and have them die in some sort of plane crash. Something along those lines. Did you know he doesn't even carry a cell phone? What person does that? Whatever. You work on making sure everyone is on the plane, then get me the flight and such so I can have it taken care of. This is a matter of most importance. The man is dirty, and I want him out of the picture."

"You said you wanted him dead for gain." Did he? He didn't remember that but nodded. "What's your angle on this? I'm not going to kill a good man simply because you want to get your name out there in a better light for the upcoming election. My job is reconnaissance, not target and kill."

"You'll do what you're told, or you might be on the plane too. I won't have a problem making sure your body is there when the rest of them are found. Just watch yourself, young lady, or you'll find yourself out of a life." He was quite proud of his little comeback until she called him a moron. Again. "You come here and confront the president of the United States, and you don't think I'll pull strings to have you taken care of as well? You're barking up the wrong tree, Rising Star. What sort of name is that, anyway? Not that it matters. I know now what you look like, and I'll find you if I have to go to the ends of the earth to do so."

"You're very into idioms, aren't you? Well, here's one for you, Mike Waller. You don't know shit. As soon as I walk away, you not only won't be able to recall what I look like, but you won't have any idea what you said to me. Again, not much of a hardship since you can't even remember to zip your fly when you leave the bathroom."

He wasn't going to check. Mike wasn't going to give her the satisfaction of him finding that it was indeed zipped up. Her laughter made him think of chimes in the wind and nails on a chalkboard at the same time. Looking around the cemetery, he looked back at the woman. Not only was she gone, but his wife was standing there.

"What the hell are you doing?" He said he was talking to a woman on the fence about voting for him. "What woman? You've been out here for an hour talking to this headstone like some kind of fruit. I told the ladies you were praying. You'd better be praying for something, Mike. Ellen just got arrested for trying to kill Jamison. We need to get out of here, now."

They left, and he was worried sick what the hell was going to happen now. The woman. That's all he could think about. What did she look like? Who was she? Was there a woman? His mind was a complete mess of jumbled thoughts as he made his way back to the living quarters of his home. When he could, Mike slipped away to go to his little, quiet office. He nearly shit his pants when he saw that not only was the safe open, but the thing was devoid of anything other than an envelope with his name on it.

With shaking fingers, he opened it up. Dropping to the floor, the note fell from his fingers as the two words kept circling in his head. *You're next. You're next. You're next.*

Mike searched the office for over an hour, looking for any kind of clue that would tell him what he'd done. Had he left the safe open? Did someone come in here that shouldn't have? The marine that guarded the room from all intruders said no one had come in on his watch. For some reason, he didn't believe him. As he made his way up to his rooms, Mike had a sudden thought. Had he been recorded in the cemetery? If so, who had the recordings now? Christ, he was so fucked. And he didn't have the first clue what he'd done to do it to himself.

There were seventeen messages when he went by his personal desk. They were all from Jamison, and he needed to call him right back, no matter the time. It was nearly midnight now, but he called the man. He was as frantic as he'd ever heard him be.

"She came at me with a knife, Mike. Just kept telling me I was next. Next at what, I had no idea. They're going to put her away for a few days. Someone said she acted like she was stoned or something. Do you suppose she's added that to the shit she's been doing?" Mike told him he didn't know. He decided not to tell him about the note he'd received. "Then after she stabbed

Kathi S. Barton

me in the arm twice, she just fell to the floor and started sobbing about someone making her do it. Mike, I was with her all evening, and there hadn't been a soul around for hours. What the hell is going on?"

"I don't know. Someone came to see me at the gala tonight. I can't recall what was said between us, nor what the person looked like. I mean, I don't remember now if it was a male or female. Then just now, I realized I didn't even check for any kind of recording devices. What the hell is going on with this shit?" Jamison said he didn't know, but he was going to be laying low for a few days. "I believe I will as well. I was going to have the Griffin family come out for dinner one night soon to honor their son, but I think I'll hold off on that as well."

He knew Jamison would understand why he was bringing them out here. When they hung up a few minutes later after Mike telling him he'd go see him soon, he sat there and tried to think what was really going on. Something surely was. But what?

The longer he sat there, the more confused he was. Finally, getting up to go to bed, he was glad to see that Emma was asleep. There wouldn't be any kind of argument between them tonight.

Changing his clothing for pajamas, he decided that he'd had a brain fart. That was all it had been.

Getting into bed, he really didn't feel any better about the way he was feeling, so he took a couple of sleeping pills and hoped they'd work for him. It was strange, he thought, that things were falling apart right now. Like he was being watched all the time, and someone knew his every move.

Mike rolled over. There was no way anyone could get to him. He was the fucking president of the United States. People would die for him. However, he wasn't so sure about that anymore. Closing his eyes, Mike let the drugs take him under. It was that, or he was going to be in deep shit when he had to go to the Oval Office. He wasn't sure he could get there at this point.

The dreams were vivid and full of color. He remembered being really sick about what he was seeing, but he didn't wake. There was blood and bones everywhere like there had been a massacre, and he'd been watching it unfold from the sidelines. Until he saw a mirror. Why there was a mirror on a field of the dead, he had no idea. But with one look at himself, he knew that whatever the dream was telling him, he'd been the one that had killed all the people.

You didn't kill them, per se. However, you did have a great deal to do with it. That's going to be your biggest fame from being president. The one thing that is brought up every time your name is mentioned. Which won't be all that often, as you'll be stricken from history books, and it'll be considered taboo for anyone to think of you in a good way. Now that, I know, won't be a problem. He looked around for the person speaking. *I'm not with you but in your head. You have a lot of information up there in the empty cavern that I've been able to use against you. Did you really kill your own parents? Shame on you.*

Who is this? The voice only laughed. Not even with that clue did he know anything about them. *I demand that you show yourself. Tell me who you are.*

Oh goody. I was hoping you'd demand something. Do you remember that Disney movie where the little wooden boy had a cricket? You can think of me as that cricket. I'm going to be right there with you all the time from now on, pointing out your misdeeds. I figure I'll be working nonstop, but it'll be worth it to drive you over the edge. I can do it, too. I've gotten that good. Oh, by the way, did you see your safe? It was both kind and stupid of you to leave such an easy combination for me to get into it. Some people are smart enough to make it really difficult. But not you. You're forever looking for an easy way out, aren't you, Mikey? He told her that he was Mr. President to her. *Not for long, you're not. And to think I had high hopes of your partner being killed by his wife, then her coming after you. Oh well, I'll do better the next time.*

What is it you want from me? I have money. I'll pay you off. She told him he'd *had* money, both he and Jamison. *What is that supposed to mean? I'd better have my money.*

You don't. I'm going to rest now. Big day for tomorrow. You behave yourself until I can get back to you, Mikey. Damn it. I forgot to tell you this at the first. Your wife is dead. I didn't have anything to do with it, but she'd killed herself. Or at least that's what it looks like. If I were you, I'd try and find the drugs she took before she cut her wrists right there in the bed with you before the police arrive. I don't think you'll be able to wake her in time, but I did warn you. They'll have your prints all over them since you've been getting them for her. So will the knife, I suppose. Good night, Mikey. TTYL. In the event you don't know what that means, it means "talk to you later." This is going to be so much fun for me.

Mike was shaken awake—hard too—and the sun was shining brightly into his bedroom.

The man standing over him didn't look familiar, but he was still trying to wake up. Before he could figure out what he was saying to him, Mike was jerked from the bed and asked to stand up. It took him a few minutes to remember the dream he'd had. The agent, or whoever he was, asked him a million questions in a matter of seconds. It was then he noticed that he was not only covered in blood, but his bed was as well.

"Mr. President, can you tell us what happened here? What happened to the first lady?" He could only stare at the bed. "Mr. President? Can you tell us what — ?"

"They said she killed herself?" He asked him who had said that. "I don't know. The person in my head. They said I needed to wake up so I could find the drugs."

It took him all of a split second to realize what he was saying. Sure it was too late, he closed his mouth, only opening it to ask for his attorney. Christ, he'd played right into their hands, whoever they were, and now he'd just admitted not only that he was insane but that there were drugs in the personal home of the president of the US.

Chapter 6

Turning themselves in seemed their best course of action. George didn't like it any better than Linda did, but they were hungry, cold, and most of the time without even a place to take a piss, much less a clean place to lie down. Finding either of their daughters proved to be impossible. And even if they were able to find them, what the hell would they look like standing in front of them in their bathing suits, now a mess for wearing just them over the last three days? What the hell would they do that wouldn't have them laughing at them for hours? Nothing, that was what. Besides, he thought Linda had a point in them not working and owing taxes.

"We'll do it today." She stood up. "Not right at this moment, Linda. We're going to have to have some sort of plan, don't you think?"

"A plan? All right, I have a plan. We're going to go to the police station, tell them who we are, and wait for someone to feel sorry for us, or for that matter, smell us, and they'll let us have a shower, clothing, and a good meal. Even condemned people get better than we've had for the last few days, George. Hell, even our stupid son has it better than we do right now, and he's locked away from other people. Fuck this shit. We do this now. Planning went out the window when those wolves or dogs or whatever the hell they were came at us with their fur standing up on end and biting the shit out of us."

"We don't want to go in there without any kind of plan, Linda. What if they ask us where we got the money? Or, for that matter, why weren't we paying taxes on the houses? We could lose them both. Then where would we be?" She said she didn't care. "You will when they take our place to live."

"I just don't care, George. Can't you see how bad we look? When was the last time you had any food? Longer than we should have gone, I'm telling you that right now. I'm starving. Just looking at dumpsters makes me salivate." He told her that was disgusting. "Of course it is, you moron. I was making a point as to how hungry I am. We're going in. Tell them to leave us alone. That this is harassment and that we're going home. At this point, being in jail is preferable to this shit right here. And when we're out — there isn't any way they'll be able to hold us for long — we'll think of another plan and get the girls to get their shit together and get us out of this mess. If you think about it, you'll see that this is the only way we can put this behind us."

George didn't think there was any way the girls were going to help them now. They were different than before. Even as dense as he was about women and love, he could see that they were as happy as they'd ever been and seemed to glow with this newfound whatever. Standing up, handing the blanket to his wife, they made their way out of the barn. As soon as they cleared the doorway, the man that had been around his daughters every time he'd seen them was there standing by a brand-new car. The temporary tags were still on it, along with the sticker sheet.

"You ready to call it quits and go to jail?" Linda was making her way to the car, her head nodding like it was broken or something. "I'll take you that way, so I'm assured that you get there. By the way, you should know your home in California has been taken for lack of payments on the taxes."

"At this point, we just don't care." George said nothing as Linda got into the back seat. "Come on, George. You just said this is what you wanted to do. This man is going to take us there, so we don't have to walk. My feet are still bleeding from yesterday."

He didn't get in but stood there staring at the man. "You're in love with Storm, aren't you?" Edwin, he thought his name was, nodded and smiled. "Yes, I can see that now. It's nothing I've ever seen so brilliantly on someone before. Will you be taking care of Rain too? She's sort of lost without her sister."

"You care?" George told him he had no idea what he felt anymore. "Yes, I can see that on your face. I don't know what you mean by Rain being lost without her sister, but she's a good deal stronger than you might have thought. In fact, she's stronger than Storm on some things. I don't think you'd be able to push her around anymore. She'd not let you."

"I believe you." Nodding, the man stood there. "But you'll take care that they're both safe? From people like us? I haven't any idea why that keeps pounding at my head that I want them to be safe from predators like us, but I need to hear you say that."

"They'll be safe, I promise you that. Rain has a better outlook on life. And as I said, is stronger than before. Storm is also stronger, in love with me, and we'll marry soon. The two of you, you'll never be a part of their lives if you don't get your head out of your asses and turn yourselves around. Regardless, I'm going to have children with Storm if she wishes. I'm hoping that Rain finds herself someone to love her as much as I love her sister. I think that's more than either of them would have had if you were to be a part of their lives." He realized the man was right and said as much. "If you don't mind me asking, what changed your mind about them?"

George looked at the car and noticed that the door was now closed. What he said to this man wouldn't be overheard by Linda. This might well be his only opportunity to talk straight forward to him.

"A dream I had. A man—I can't recall that much about him, nor do I know him even now—showed me some things we've done to our kids that I'm ashamed of. I have no idea why at the time, I ever even thought that what we were doing was right by either of them. Nor us, for that matter." He looked away, ashamed even now at some of the things they'd said and done. "Rain was so timid…no, that's not right. She was broken for what we'd done to her. I'm not going to let my wife take all the blame, but I think she led me around by my dick most of our lives together. Sex and women are a lethal combination to some men, like me anyway. Storm too, for a time. But she seemed to understand a good deal quicker, before she became like Rain, that we were monsters. I can say that now. We were monsters, and we don't deserve to be in their lives."

"You don't." Nodding, he started to open the door again, but Edwin put his hand onto his. "I don't want to like you, George. Not one bit. But if you keep this up, I'll go to bat for you on this. Your wife, too, if you can convince her to back off. But I will help you any way I can if you are serious in what you're saying to me right now."

"I am. My wife? I don't think that'll be possible, Edwin. It might, but I don't think so. However, I've figured out that I've been wrong about a great many things about myself and Linda for a great long time now." Getting into the car, Linda asked him what had taken so long, and

George decided to tell her the truth, something he'd not done in a very long time. After telling her everything he'd said and wanted from Edwin, she snorted at him. "You don't think I can be a changed man? Or is it that you don't think you could be a changed woman?"

"I don't want to change, George. I love my life just the way it is." She looked at him, and he could see things he'd not before. She was looking her age. He supposed they both were, but there were lines of age on her that he'd never seen before. "You'll see that I'm right in this. Once we get out of jail and things are back to the way they were before, you'll see I'm right. Aren't I always right when it comes to the girls? You'll see."

"You said that a lot during our marriage, didn't you? That you were right?" She told him that was because she *was* right all the time. "I see. I guess I should have taken more notice. Because all I can see right now is that we've both fucked up. A great deal. And now we're more than likely not going to see any grandchildren we might have had."

"Grandchildren? Holy Christ, George. We definitely don't want any of those running around. That will make us really old. No. We'll have to convince them they don't want anything like that." She actually shivered. "Grandchildren. No, I do not want someone calling me Grandma like I'm some octogenarian."

He knew that neither of them were that old, but he did have to think about how old he was. Christ, he thought, he was nearly sixty-six. Other than his daughters, he had absolutely nothing at all to show for it either. He looked in the rearview mirror as the car moved out onto the road and saw Edwin was looking at him. Nodding once, he hoped the man understood that he was going to do his best to be the man he should have been decades ago. Before it was too late. Not just for him, but to be in his daughters' lives too.

By the time they'd gotten to the precinct, he was ready to confess to murdering anyone just to get out of the car and get some peace and quiet from Linda. There wasn't even any music on to drown out her voice while they rode back to town. That was another thing he'd realized — she was forever talking about anything and everything that popped into her head. Getting out of the car almost as soon as it rolled to a stop, he was going up the stairs to do whatever was required of him just to get away from her.

"Mr. Hudson?" Nodding, he told the man

in the suit that he'd do and go wherever he wanted so long as he could be in a cell far from his wife. They both turned to look at Linda and Edwin when they came into the door. Linda was still chattering like a gibbon monkey. "Yes, sir. I can do that for you. I believe it'll be no trouble at all."

They were both standing there when they were cuffed. Of course, Linda had to have something to say about that. George just put out his hands and let them do whatever they wanted. The more he thought about what he was doing, the more he thought he was doing the right thing with all of this, including the thing with his wife.

Read his rights now. He was taken to a room. There was a large ring in the table, but he wasn't attached to his as he thought he would have been. Sitting there, he thought of his daughters, Storm especially. She'd forever been one of the most beautiful women he'd ever seen, and he'd had something to do with her creation.

George didn't want to be emotional when they came back to talk to him, but he did let his mind wander on what it would be like to hold his own grandchild. A little girl like one of his daughters. Beautiful brown eyes that would seem to dance with other colors.

He remembered a time when Storm would come to him in the evenings. She'd only done it a couple of times, but then no more. She'd wanted him to read to her, and he turned her away because he'd wanted some quiet time. Even then, he came to remember, Linda had talked all the time. Still, that had been no excuse to turn a child away that had wanted to spend time with him.

Rain, too, would come to him when she'd been hurt, a boo-boo on her knee or one at her tiny elbow. It didn't occur to him when they'd stopped coming. George only remembered a time when they'd left him alone. That they no longer bothered him, a word a parent should never use referring to one of his children.

There were other things he came to remember while sitting there all alone. Not just to do with his children, but just life in general. He'd had a college education. George had done very well in both school and college. Why hadn't he done something with that? Why hadn't he, even as intelligent as he'd been, done something more than just work a system he had no rights to, as well as using his namesakes?

Then there was Georgie. It had been Linda's fault he was born the way he was. The doctors had told her she needed to stop drinking. That smoking wasn't just harming her, but the baby as well. He had taken a stand against her during that time, leaving her once to get her to understand how serious he was about her having a healthy child.

She had stopped, or so he had thought. All during the pregnancy, she'd been doing both drinking to the point where she was out of touch with life and smoking to the point where he should have picked up on it. Linda would get up in the middle of the night and drink all through the night, she'd told him after Georgie was born. Then, before George got up, she'd get back into the bed, drunk out of her mind, and sleep the rest of the day away, telling him, and he stupidly thought she was telling him the truth, that she was exhausted all the time from carrying a child. When in reality, she was hungover and in a stupor.

Georgie had been born much too small. Weighing in at just under four pounds, his lungs were underdeveloped, as was his brain. He had so much alcohol in his little body when he'd come into the world that he had to be weaned off it, much the same as an adult had to be. There were other birth defects as well. He was born with a cleft lip, no fingers on his right hand, as well as blind. The child had never stood a chance at a good life even before he'd been born. It had broken his heart when he'd seen him. Then with Linda guiding the way, he'd not thought of him again. Only little pieces of him when one of the girls were being born. He'd been a horrible person and father to all three of them.

Agent Filament came into the room just as George was coming to terms with his sad existence, as well as his poor excuse for being a human being. Christ, he nearly hurled himself at the man as soon as he sat down.

"I want the full penalty for what you're arresting me for. I don't care, even if I have to spend the rest of my life in prison. It's no less than I deserve." The agent, a young man, said he had things to go over with him. "Yes, I did it all. Linda as well, but I am guilty of a great many things you more than likely won't have on your books. I was a terrible man and the worst father ever born. Ever in the history of children being born, I was the worst."

"Unfortunately, I can't put you in prison for being a terrible person or father, Mr. Hudson. Mr. Griffin, Edwin, said that if you cooperated, he'd help you with the court costs. But I'm to ask you if your wife will want to cooperate as well." George told him he doubted she'd want to have anything to do with him after today. "She is someone that needs to blame others, isn't she? But that's not the point. There are charges pending against the two of you for which it will go a long way in reducing your sentencing if you were to cooperate with us. And answer a few questions too."

The questions were put to him one at a time. George had had to ask for a pen and paper so he could write them down so he could remember to add things to them as he got around to remembering things that he couldn't at the time. Drinks were brought to him as he sat there. He was using his fifth sheet of paper when Paul, the agent, asked him if he wanted to take a break for some dinner. George hadn't even realized so much time had passed.

After dinner was brought to him, George told him some of the things he'd done in the name of his girls. Credit cards taken out with false information. His treatment of them when they'd been small. Even telling the man about how he'd locked them in closets or in the basement when they wouldn't help them.

Never once did he say anything that had

been done was Linda's idea when in reality, some of it had been. He was ready to take full blame for everything. Anything, really, to set his life on the road to where he thought he deserved to be.

Tissues had been brought to him when he'd lost control of his emotions. Once, he'd been so upset that Paul had come around to the other side of the table and hugged him, holding him as he sobbed out again and again what a terrible person he'd been. Then when he was ready to begin anew, Paul would give him a few minutes to gather himself up so he could tell it all.

That night, exhausted beyond anything he'd ever felt before, George went to bed feeling like a new person. Not a better one, but new all the same. He'd gotten a great many things off his chest, and he'd been able to tell someone what sort of things he'd done, in the name of being a father, to two of the best children in the world. Paul, thankfully, never once told him he was just what he thought he was.

~*~

Edwin came in the door and put his keys in the bowl by the door. The house felt different. As he was just about to go into the kitchen for something to hold him over till breakfast, Rain came out of the living room and smiled at him.

"I've just called for Storm. She's been working since you called. You have a visitor. He's been talking to me, said he knew your dad, but he's not once told me why he's here. His name is Romeo. That's all he said." The name was familiar, but not one he could recall as to why he knew it. "He said you'd need to call your parents here. That they'd be able to help him explain a great deal."

"Romeo Hank." Rain said he'd never told her his last name. "I think he is my grandfather. I mean, sort of. I'll call my parents right now."

After reaching out to them, his mom and dad said they were on their way. Even though it was nearly eleven, Dad said he was up anyway. Dad had been an early riser and going to bed with the sun all his life. Whatever was going on, Dad seemed to have been prepared for it. Going into the living room, he looked at the man sitting on his couch.

"Hello, Edwin. My goodness, you certainly are as handsome as I knew you'd be. Did you call your parents and wife to us yet?" He said he had and that they were on their way. "Yes, they would want some answers after all this time. I heard you tell that lovely young woman there that you thought I was your grandfather. If you think that, then you're aware that I am only in that position because I helped change your parents into what they are today."

"I don't know anything about you other than you left him alone when you were to help him transition into being the leader of a pack but didn't." Romeo said there was a reason for that. "I hope so, but I have a feeling that with or without your help, my dad did a better job of keeping the pack in good standing than he would have had you been around."

"I've no doubt about that. He was and is a good person. Your mother too." Edwin held onto Storm when she came into the room with him. "You're beautiful, young lady. As beautiful as a sunrise that you've not seen for centuries. You and your sister, you've done a great deal since you were born, and I couldn't be prouder of you both."

"Proud of us? I don't know where you get off saying something like that when I've never met you before, and you've had no say in our lives." Romeo just smiled at her. "Why the hell are you here now? I'm assuming it has something to do with money or the pack. Well, you'll not get anything from this family if I have anything to say about it. They're mine now, and you'll not harm them in any way."

"No. I'd never do that. But I do have some explaining to do." The door opened behind them, and Edwin turned to hug his parents. Mom went to Romeo as the man stood. "Hello, my child. You're just what I imagined you'd look like as a human."

The punch to his face knocked the man back onto the couch and over the back. No one moved for several seconds. It was Dad that started laughing. No one joined him, however.

Dad looked over at him and hugged him. "You've no idea how many times your mother has said she wanted to knock the man out for what he did to us. I have to tell you, son. It will make her day for years to come for her being able to do this." Edwin said he didn't understand. "No, you'd not. But I think we might just have the opportunity to find out now. Let's call the others in, and we'll get this all straightened out. In the meantime, let's get this person up and going. Before your mother knocks him around a bit more."

This was the strangest night he'd ever had, he thought. First of all, he had a grandfather of sorts that he didn't even know that much about.

His mother was more violent than he'd ever imagined, which he thought she might have been all along, but needed the right buttons pushed. Then there was the fact that he had yet to make love to his mate, and he needed her in the worst sort of way. Even if he were only to hold her tightly in his arms.

His brothers showed up in good time. Chaplin did as well but sat with his mom rather than with any of the others. Edwin didn't know if it was to keep her calm or something else, but he was glad to see his mom smiling rather than looking like she was ready to do battle. When Romeo sat down again, he didn't look any worse for wear but smiled at them all. When a platter of food appeared, mostly finger stuff they could eat, Edwin didn't eat anything until Romeo did. It was just too much for him to handle on top of everything, having food appear like it was an everyday thing.

"Let me begin at the beginning. Before your father came along and just after I was created. That was, so you know, long before the earth as you know it was like it was. Many changes had come to pass before I came to your father. And I'm sad to say a great many men like him were left without a mate." Dad asked if he'd not been the first man he'd contacted to do what he needed with the pack. "Nay. You were not. However, as much as it saddens me that you weren't, I'm happy one of the men that refused to take a part of the life I offered him went on and had children of his own."

Edwin looked at Rain and Storm then. "You're saying that somewhere back in their lineage, their ancestor was someone you tried to take over for you?" Romeo nodded and smiled at him. "So we're related?"

"Oh no. No." Romeo looked at him. "The man that was to take over for me then had been given the same magic I gave your father. Not my seed, as you think, but simply magic. When he thought himself not a good enough man to take over, I never thought to take back the magic that had been given to him. I only waited until the next man came along so I could try again. Your father was the third such man. But this man, the one that went on to have his own family, he passed the magic, as it was only magic, down to his own heirs. It only manifested in the children of George and Linda. In the magic I left with him was a bit of the wolf, too, so that he'd be able to shift and run with the pack. Again, I never thought to take it back. For which, I'm very glad that I didn't."

"You went to see him, didn't you? My father. You talked to him." Romeo said he had. "You had him change his mind in what he'd been planning to do to Rain and I."

"I only showed him what he'd done to the two of you when you were with him. Then beyond, to what had happened to the two of you because of it. I never once blamed it on him and only him. However, he did take full responsibility for the actions that were done by both your parents." Storm asked how she was supposed to trust anyone after what he'd done to her dad. "You will come to trust me or not, Storm. That will be up to you. However, I can tell you this, and you can believe it or not, but it was your mother that led your father by the dick, as he has said to me himself, and caused the trouble that happened to his daughters. He should have been a better man and might well have been had it not been for her influence. But he was an adult and could have, and I think should have, gotten out of her web long before I came to see him."

"Romeo, I'd like you to start at the beginning. I want to know everything." Rain looked at Storm. "You want to know how we began, don't you? I know it would make me feel better just knowing I'm not some freak of whatever all this is. Wouldn't you?"

"Yes. But I'm not happy about what has gone on." Romeo said she should be, as without what had happened to her, she'd never have met Edwin, nor would she have the magic to pass on down to her own children. "What if I don't want them to have the magic you gave my ancestor?"

"Oh, but you will want that. And more. Your children will come to be very powerful in the world around us. Great leaders and will come to be sought after by all means of people. Rain, you as well." Romeo looked at Rain as he spoke. "Your own mate is around even now. A good man that will come to cherish you as much if not more than Edwin does his own mate. Much more so than the coming mates to the other boys of Charlie and my Luna."

"Will they bring magic as well?" Romeo told Tony when he asked that they'd all have magic by the time he left them again. "Will we have children of our own as well?"

"Yes. By heart or love, you'll all have many children before you come to realize that you've given enough. There will be many people that will come into your hearts that will forever praise the things you've done for them. That you've, by no other reason than just being a part of their lives, made them go on to be much better people than they had been. Your father, Rain, he will also become someone that will do a great many things for a lot of people."

"I'm ready." They all looked at Storm when she spoke. "Tell us it all. I need to know, I think, so I can do whatever it takes to make sure the world in which we all live is a safer and better place than it is now."

"Good for you, young lady." Romeo looked at Mom before he spoke again. "When I found Luna, she was nothing more than a pup, starved by being alone for so long. She was near death when I happened upon her one bright afternoon. I'd found my child, my hope for the pack I was caring for since I'd been put upon the earth to make the first shifter wolf. Men and wolves that would change the way things were going for them so they'd not be just a small blot on the world we all know."

Chapter 7

Romeo thought about the things he was telling this family. Some of it Luna knew. A great deal of it, she did not like how he'd come to be. And that, he thought, was the crux of everything that had come to pass, her lack of knowledge about what she was and how she'd come to be his dearest creation.

"When I was nothing more than a small seed floating upon the air, I could see the need for changes. Not just in the wolves, who were at one time such a hunted and hated group of beings. I was sent to take care that there were shifters, of all kinds, that could make a stand for themselves and others, as well as keeping them safe from even themselves." Charlie asked him if he'd had a hand in other shifters. "Yes. For the most part. I was more of the creator of the first of their kind into shifting men and women. After that, the magic that made them be able to become human was there for them to have. It was, as you can imagine, something that had to be decided back in the day. It was, like your predecessor, something they had to decide to take. Lucky for all of the wolves around, you took on the role that you were suited for."

He looked around before continuing. "The first man I encountered was a good man. However, he never felt in his heart that he was anything more than a broken man that had nothing to offer such a project. Sadly, after he walked away, he was found dead. Not by his own hand, but by another that thought he had more than him. Which he did, as it turned out, but nothing that the man could take. The second man was your ancestor, Storm and Rain, as you have figured out on your own. He was, like Charlie and the man before him, a great man. Smart as well. But he thought himself to be nothing more than a man and wanted no part of it." Storm said this wasn't the start. "No, I suppose it isn't. All right. I was created by the queen of all earth. She wanted the world to be better, as you can well imagine. But to do that, she'd need help in the form of the shifters. So I was created by magic. Not just the sort that a witch might have, but from all the elements of mankind. Water, air, earth, and fire. Which, I'm thinking, all of you can now use."

He didn't wait for them to try it out but pulled the four elements out of the air and showed them how he'd been made. A little of each of the elements to create what he was now. He looked over in time to see Storm do the same, creating a small speck of what she could do in the form of a globe of magic. She put it into the air, and when it rained down onto the carpet, what was left was the creation of not just him but the queen herself.

He watched in awe as he was made. Never had he seen it, as he'd not been able to form memories from that time. As he was put together with the four things he knew of, there were other things added to his speck in the form of other creatures. All of them, he came to see.

Then as he watched, not only was his formation created, but Romeo saw his life, in starts and jerks, being relived right before his eyes. He realized then that he'd been wrong about the two women. Storm was a great deal stronger of the two of them. Not only that, but he knew her to be much stronger than even he was.

I got tired of waiting on you. Storm smiled at him as she spoke in his mind. *You'll see that I'm not one to be patient with things I want answers to.*

I can see that. He looked back at the night Charlie had come to him. "This, this is the reason I couldn't come back to help my new family with the taking over of the pack."

Charlie had been shot — twice, as a matter of fact. The wound to his chest was bad, but it was the one to his head that did the most damage. Romeo watched as his future in the form of Charlie bled out on the ground.

"He had sent Luna back to warn the pack of the men coming. Had he not done that, I would never have been able to get to him in time. As it was then, I called on the earth to help shield him from any more harm. Once he was as safe as he could be, with the others scattered to keep the men from killing them all, I made my way to him to do what I needed to save him." Storm asked him if it was the unselfish act that had brought him to him. "It was. Yes. It was just that. You see, had he not done what he did, all the pack would have perished in one way or another. The males would have died, and the females would never have been able to recover. The pack would have eventually died off, and that would have been the end of all wolf shifters. I had to save him, at a great cost to my own magic."

They all watched as he went to the younger man and gave him all he had to spare, leaving him with nothing more than a small amount of magic, which was what he needed to be put to rest until recently.

"Why now?" Romeo asked Luna what she meant. "You could have come back sooner, I'm assuming. Why didn't you come to us and explain before now?"

"Because he was awakened by the earth." Rain stared at him. "I didn't call for you when I was in the yard. I only asked for information. Something that would explain, even to myself, what the hell I was here for. Then, I'm assuming you took care of a couple of things—my dad being one of them—so you'd be able to explain what happened to make us what we are today. You went to see him."

"Yes. That's right. I was drawn to him when I realized I might well have left things in a mess by not taking the magic from your first relative with magic. I'm ever so glad I didn't, but as you can tell, it was something I thought to take care of. However, it turned out much differently than I had thought it would." Storm said it was because he had found them. "Yes. I found that you two had been born with all the magic that had been left to him. And in turn, you somehow were able to gather all the magic that had been passed down, and it made you what you both are. Strong magic. Stronger magic than even I have."

"Good." They both laughed when Storm said that. "What I mean is, we'll be able to help with the family from now on. To not just keep them safe—not that I don't think they could do that on their own—but keep them all from anything that might come their way."

The conversation went on until the sun came up. Still, they seemed to be ready for answers, some of which he didn't have. But he was enjoying himself, even after Charlie and Luna went to their home to rest, with a promise from him that he'd be there for some time now, if not forever. He wasn't their relative, but he'd never felt a part of anything until this very moment. Family, he realized, was what he'd been missing all his life.

Before Luna left, he'd asked her if he could stay as a part of her family. She only stared at him before turning to her boys—grown men really, but she still obviously thought of them as boys. When she turned back to him, he wasn't at all sure what she was going to say to him.

"You must ask my boys." He asked her why he had to do that, just looking at the men standing there, looking to protect their mother at all costs, not to mention harming him in the process. "Because I said so. They'll be the ones that will have to keep you in line should you wish to make trouble while you're here. And we both know you like to cause trouble when you have nothing to keep you busy. And with them, I believe they'll keep you busy enough that trouble will never haunt you again."

He wanted to point out that she'd keep him out of trouble just fine, but he wasn't going to push her buttons just yet. Romeo would do that later when it was just the two of them. Teasing her had been enough for him when they'd been looking for her Charlie. Wondering what had changed her mind, he tried his best to bond with the boys of his Luna.

"No." He looked at Storm when she spoke. "I don't know what you're thinking, and to be honest, I don't really care. You'll behave yourself, or I'll rain such a pile of shit down on your head that you'll regret every being created.

Do you understand me?"

Romeo might have teased her, but Rain was right behind her sister. He had a feeling the reference to *raining* something down on his head wasn't a coincidence. Rain would help her with the pile.

Since he had no home to go to, he fixed himself a place in the yard. It was a nice little house, more like a small shed. However, once he was inside, it looked like a place he could spend the rest of his days in. Also be able to be around his adopted family.

By the time he'd made as many changes as he thought he might need, Romeo made his way to his garden, a thing that he had with him no matter where he went. It was a place of quiet, reflection, and also a place he knew he'd share company with the little faeries that had been his since the day he'd become a magical being.

"Sir, I have some information on the two families from the White House. They have been in business with their misdeeds for longer than they have been in office. Lady Storm and Lady Rain have been very thorough. Had it not been for them, I fear that all we've worked for with the place of government would have been for nothing." He asked where they were now. "They're both in jail. The Mrs. President is deceased. I don't know what drove her to it, but it is done, and that is one less thing we must worry about. Are you certain the Lady Rain will make a good mate to Agent Filament that will be working with her?"

"I do. I foresee things coming for the two of them that will help a great many creatures of this earth." Chaplin nodded and seemed to be staring off into the plants, but Romeo knew him to be seeing what the future would bring. "Do you see it?"

"I do, my lord. I will think on one or two of the small ones here to work with her. I believe she will need it more than most." Romeo agreed with him to sort that out. "I shall stay with Lady Luna. She and I have been together off and on for some time. Without her knowledge, of course. But I was there to help her with a guiding hand. She was a good deal easier to work with than some other magical creatures I know."

"Yes, but we did have some fun." They had, even though Chaplin huffed at him. "If you'd take care of the small ones and make sure they're a good match, I can not worry about that for now. However, there are a couple of more things I'd like to discuss with you."

They spent the better part of the day working on plans that had been set in motion long ago. Neither of them needed to sleep to rest, just a few glasses of juice or even a bit of the flowers that were in his gardens.

The only thing they would have to work into their plans was the magic the two women had brought with them when they'd come to the family. Romeo was very certain the magic they had with the magic he was giving to the others was going to make the Griffins the most powerful beings ever made, born or created. Keeping the shifters of all kinds safe would most assuredly be a good thing forever.

After Chaplin left him to begin his work, Romeo called for the queen of the earth. She appeared just as young and beautiful as he'd ever seen her. With his help, he knew her job was a great deal less than it had been. Romeo thought she looked younger because of it.

"Don't get your head into more trouble than you can handle, Romeo. I have enough on my plate at the moment." He told her what he'd discovered with the young women. "So, they have been able to gather all the magic of their lineage to use. That is quite a bit, don't you think?"

"More than I have, I believe. I will try and balance out the magic they have with the Griffins, but I doubt it will make much of a difference. They're strong, as I said, and it would drain me to make it work." She said she'd take care of it. "Then might I make a suggestion? A small one. Don't balance them at all. Give the men magic, as much as you wish. But I'd leave Storm to be stronger. Rain as well, but Storm will be the one that will wield it to care for them all. They have good heads on their shoulders and enough smarts to know when to use the magic and not. Not that the Griffins won't, but they'd be calmer about it."

"I will take that under advisement. I like the idea, but I will have to see what things are to come to pass with all of this. Have you been able to locate the parents?" He told her what he'd been able to do for the father. "Can you make it so he is able to stay here without prison? I should like to see them have a parent around when they need it. I don't know anything about the missus, but from what I can see in your mind, she has no redeemable qualities about her. That, I think, would cause more trouble with the magic the daughters have than not. Don't you agree?"

"I believe she will need to be put away for

a long time. You are aware of the child of them both, are you not? How he is handicapped badly from her misdeeds before the child was born?" She touched his mind, and he could see when she found the information. "What would you like for me to do about her? She will continue to be a bad influence on them all should she be allowed to live beyond the prison walls."

"I will think on that." She stood up and smiled at him. "You're a good man, Romeo. A pain in my bottom, yes, but a good man all around. I heard the exchange between you and Luna. It did my heart good to hear her putting you in your place. All right. I must go. You let me know when you've decided what to do about the small ones. I will contact you when I have the information on the mother."

"Thank you, my lady."

Romeo bowed before her, and when he felt her leave him, he stood up. Going into his garden, he talked with the creatures there and made his decisions for the family. Yes, Romeo thought, he was going to have to keep on his toes with these new family dynamics, and he was looking forward to it.

~*~

Exhaustion had never felt so good. Edwin

had a lot more information than he thought his dad had before tonight. As he was stripping down to his skin, the door opened, and Storm slipped into his room.

"I'm too tired to move, but I want to feel your body next to mine. Do you care?" He shook his head, then nodded. "I can leave. Or you can use your words. What do you want?"

"You. But like you, I'm exhausted as well. Come on. Get into…I don't have any sleepwear." She just laughed as she started to take off her clothing as well. "Well then, I guess we don't care about that."

They talked about the information but didn't put too much effort into coming to any kind of resolution about what it would mean to them. Storm went into the bathroom, and when she came out, she got into the bed. He did the same but didn't walk around to the other side. He got in on the same side she was on.

"This bed is very nice." Edwin told her that was why he slept on it. "Don't be an ass. I only meant it was nice because you're in it with me. I love you, Edwin. I want to spend the rest of my life with you raising children and being loved. But right now, turn off the light and shut your mouth."

He was still laughing when he did just that. Rolling to his side, Storm spooned her body to his, and he held her. Yes, he thought, she was right. The bed was much nicer because they were in it together.

It was dark when he woke up. Edwin knew it had been early morning when they'd gotten into bed, so waking in the dark shouldn't have been a surprise. Sitting up, he wondered if something had awakened him or if he'd just woken up. Storm coming out of the bathroom with a toothbrush in her mouth startled him. Not just that, but she was very pregnant.

"I was wondering if you were going to get up and call your mom. She said she'd come and stay with the kids, right?" He nearly asked her how many they had, but she went back into the bathroom. She spoke to him from there. "The midwife is on her way too. Do you suppose she'll tell everyone what we have before we get to again?"

"Storm?" She came out of the bathroom. He looked at her and could see that she was more beautiful than he'd ever seen her before. "I love you, love. With all my heart. I will love you for the rest of the sunrises and sunsets that we have together."

"That was wonderful, Edwin." She started to cry, and he got up to hold her. "I'm afraid of this birthing. I know the doctor said things were just fine, but I still worry. I've never had three at one time before. I've been resting and everything like he said, but I'm so tired all the time, and I don't want you to think I'm neglecting you."

"Never that. I know you, honey. You'd never do anything to harm any of our children." Again, he wanted to ask her how many they had but didn't want to upset her again. "You lie down, and I'll see to the others. Mom will be here soon. I'll just make sure she's coming."

As soon as he left the bedroom, he knew things had changed. That he was, for some reason, at a different point in his life. When two people came toward him, he realized that he was dressed in jeans and a T-shirt. The man hugged him tightly and called him Dad.

Edwin didn't know how to react to having a man call him Dad. When the woman called him Edwin, he had a feeling she was his future daughter-in-law. That, and the fact that his son was looking at the very pregnant woman much the same way he looked at Storm, made him think he was either already a grandda, or he was about to be one. Storm came out of the bedroom behind him and hugged the couple. She also called him Eddie.

Then, in a blink of an eye, he was in his bed with Storm again. Carefully he got up and looked around. It was then that he saw Chaplin at the window of the room. It was dark out, so the only way he'd been able to see the little man was by the sparkle of his wings from the moonlight shining on them.

"You've had a bit of the future shown to you, my lord." He said he didn't understand it. "Nay, you'd not be able to tell that right now. You won't until it comes to the time you'll need to remember."

"Storm was going to have triplets. Then a man and a woman came down the hall. The man, he called me Dad. The woman was large with a child of their own." Chaplin came to land on his knee when he sat down on the edge of the bed. "Can you tell me what is going to happen?"

"No. I don't know. I wouldn't, as it was your future." He nodded. "I can tell you that you'll know what needs to be done with those images when they come to you in life. Perhaps it will be nothing more than a simple hug. Or that you might need to make sure your son is here when the child you said she was carrying comes.

As I said, I don't know."

"That was helpful." He looked around this room. "This room, it's the same in the future, now that I think on it. However, the hallway isn't. It was larger. Grander, I think it would be called."

If Chaplin knew anything, he wasn't saying. It would just be too much for them to know about their own future, his mom had said to him before. Sometimes it made the event coming scarier for knowing. He thought that might be the case now.

"There will be others coming to the households, sir. Little people that will help with daily tasks and the magic you'll receive. If you'd not mind me saying so, I'd allow Romeo to stay. I think it will be good for him to be around strong people. And those women—" Chaplin laughed hard. "They'll keep him in line too. He's a bit of a troublemaker when he's not watched."

"There will be other women too, I guess." He nodded. "You're very closed mouthed, aren't you, Chaplin? Is that on purpose, or are you always like this?"

"I can tell you about each of them if you were to ask me. But again, I think you would be less excited about their coming if you did know. Then there is the fact that you'd be knowing things about them and your brothers that you might not really wish to know and understand. It's better, I believe, to leave it as it lies." Yes, he supposed he was right in that. "You should retire back to the bed, my lord. It will be morning again soon, and you and the missus, you have a great deal to take care of."

Before he could think about getting into bed, he found himself there. Sitting up again, the room was dark as before, but he could see a little of the sunlight starting to show itself. Deciding that he was going to lay there until Storm woke, he curled his body around hers and closed his eyes. Whatever happened from here on out, he decided he was going to let it flow as it should. There wasn't really anything he could do about it until it came.

The next time he opened his eyes, it was to see Storm over him, riding his cock like she'd been at it a while. Pulling her down to him, Edwin kissed her with all the passion he had for her and held her tightly to him. When she lifted her head, she smiled. Edwin thought he could have powered the world with just the brilliance of it.

"You have such a lovely cock, my dear mate. I couldn't resist having a little bit of fun with you." Her whispered comments made it feel all the sexier with what she was doing to him. "Do you suppose you can make love to me? Make me scream out your name several times before we get up and going for the day?"

"Yes, I can do that. Just for you. But I'd like to come a couple of times as well." She giggled when he rolled her to her back with him between her legs. "Next time, I'll have to wake before you so I can have a tasty treat of all of you."

"Please. Edwin, please make love to me." He kissed her again, gently this time. As he made love to her mouth, he touched her anywhere he could. Her breasts were tight with need. Her nipples were thick and hard, and he sampled her there. When he nipped at the tender flesh, she cried out and told him she needed more. Stretching out over her, he held her hands above her head so he could touch her at his leisure.

Her muscles were toned and thick. Not in a manly way, but just supple enough that he knew she could take whatever was given to her. As he slid in and out of her, his cock feeling the tightness of her sheath, Edwin told her how much he loved her, in words and in touch.

For as old as he was, Edwin knew there had been none other like Storm before her. Nor would there be anyone after her that he would feel this way about. Love, he thought, had never meant anything to him like it did now. Nothing had. Not the sun rising, the earth moving. Not even a simple breeze through his hair as he walked in the early sunshine.

Edwin brought her to peak several times. It was never enough—she told him that several times. But each time she came, crying out his name, was another piece of his heart that belonged to her.

Lifting her up, so she sat on his lap, his cock buried deeply inside of her. Edwin made love to her this way, helping her ride him over and over as he suckled her breasts, bit at her flesh. When he felt her body tensing up, he laid her back down, slammed his cock deep inside of her, and watched the most wonderous thing he'd ever witnessed when she came, screaming out his name while she held him.

"Again." She shook her head but did indeed come a second, then a third time. "Storm, I love you so much."

His body seemed to steel up, harden to the point of near pain. But when he came, his body emptying into hers, he felt a renewed strength. Like making love to Storm, filling her body with his seed was all he'd been waiting for his entire life. When he came a second time, then joined her for a final climax, it was all he could do to breathe, make his heart slow enough that he could feel like he wasn't going to die when she kissed him on the nose.

"That was far and away the strangest thing you've ever done to me." She giggled as he rolled to his side, taking her with him. "You killed me there. Or I thought for sure I was going to die. What got into you?"

"You did." She laughed again. His expression must have been one of disbelief because she used her fingers to smooth out his forehead. "I'm going to have your baby soon. Not this time, but soon now. I'd like that if you would."

"Yes. Very much so." She nodded but continued to look up at him. "What is it? Did something happen?"

"Yes. I fell into a deeper love with you than I thought was possible. I love your family and want to make them mine as well. I want Rain close to us when she finds this mate of hers. Also, my dad, if we can work something out with that." He said he'd work on that with Romeo and Chaplin. "Not Chaplin. He's going to be with your mom. She is going to need someone around when she starts to feel her sons moving on. It will be hard on her to know her boys don't need her as much as they used to. You and the others, you'll have to make sure you still go to her when you need her. She'll need that more than you might realize."

"I will do that." He would, too, even if it was just to hang out with her for an afternoon making jelly or something. "What of your dad? What will you do with him? Forge a new relationship with him?"

"It will have to be new. I don't think I want to go back to the way things were before. I won't allow him to use either of us." Edwin asked her if she meant Rain. "Her as well, but you. I don't want him to come between us."

"Never that, love. I can swear to you on that score." Storm said she needed to get up, and he let her. Then, as he'd done all his life, he made his bed. As soon as the shower turned on, he went into the bathroom to brush his teeth and pull out towels for Storm. When she turned off the water, he started telling her of the day and the things they had to get moving on.

Going to the kitchen after having his own shower, he wasn't the least bit surprised to find

Paul at the table with Rain and Storm having a glass of tea. This was what family was about, and he wanted to keep these memories in his heart forever.

Chapter 8

Storm was waiting on her dad to be brought out to her when Paul came in to sit with her. She had no idea he'd be with her today and was somewhat disappointed. But he smiled and told her he was only there to tell her dad what was going to happen. Also, to tell her about the president and vice president.

"As you can well imagine, things aren't going well in DC. I've not mentioned your name. I do hope that's all right." She said she preferred it that way. "Good. I thought you might. Jamison and his wife have been arrested. The Feds have gone over their residence and have found all kinds of things there that will put them both away for a very long time. Receipts for guns. Money stashed all over the house. Other things that you might know about but aren't going to affect you. Mike has been arrested for the death of his wife. They're saying it was a suicide for now, but there is just too much evidence that shows he might well have been a part of it to let it go at that. They'll both disappear into the system and never be heard from again. I don't know that they'll live long, not with what they've done, but I'm out of it as soon as I turn over the copies of the paperwork you and Rain gave me."

"Copies." He told her why they weren't getting the originals. "I never thought of them getting rid of them so the public will never see them. So, what will you do with them now?"

"Did you know that Rain and I are mates?" She nodded. "Rain has promised me that no one will find them where she'll put them. I believe her. So should you."

"I do. Now, what about our dad?" Dad came in to sit with them just at that moment, and he wasn't chained to the table as she had thought he would have been. Instead, he reached for her hands and started sobbing about his life and how he'd done her and Rain wrong. He wanted a second chance at a life with them. "Dad, Mr. Filament has some things to say to you, then he's going to leave us. You and I will talk about what

Edwin and I are going to do for you. All right?"

"Yes, please. And thank you both." Paul explained what was going to happen and how it was going to work. There would be a trial for them both, but he was to insist that they have separate trials. "I can do that. I would love to do that."

After Paul left them, giving Dad a long list of crimes that had been committed and questions about them, Dad looked them over then looked at her. He told her he didn't know what half of them were about.

"They are counting on that, Dad. Just answer what you can and do it truthfully. Rain will be in to see you later to give you more information. She's been the one looking into the thing with you and Mom deeper than I have." He asked if she was happy. "Happy is such a mundane word for how I feel at the moment. I'm in love with a wonderful man. His family is amazing, and when you get this under your belt, we'll work on something with the three of us too. Rain is just as glad to get this started as I am. By the way, Paul is going to be seeing a great deal of Rain, so be nice to him."

"I will try and be nice to everyone I encounter from now on." Dad looked away before speaking again. "I've no right to your helping me. I was never one you could depend on. Any of you. Georgie especially. I'm going to take my share of the blame for his birth, but I will tell you that I thought she was doing what was needed to keep him healthy. I failed on so many levels as a parent."

"You did." He turned to look at her, and Storm could see the flash of anger, then the sadness. "You really didn't expect me to just say it was all right, did you? I would be really disappointed in you if you had. You fucked up on all levels at being a parent. But that doesn't mean you can't change. And really, had you been a better parent, I doubt very much that either Rain or I would be where we are today."

"I suppose that is one way to look at it. I wondered a great deal if you'd ever be able to forgive me." She told him she'd try, but it would be up to him on how that went. "What about your mother? Storm, I'm sorry about her."

"Why? You went along with her on things, and I suppose that's what you did to be with her. I'm not like that. I'll be my own watchdog with things. I have been too. But with you, until you can prove to us that you're going to be a better person, I'm going to watch you. I don't want you to be surprised by that either." He said it was no less than he expected from her. "I'm glad. Edwin and I are going to help you with court costs and getting you a good attorney. If we can, we'll pay the taxes and penalties so you won't have to do any prison time. Neither will Mom if we do that, but she has other pending charges for things she did before meeting you. So, there is more trouble on Mom's end, we'll get Mom an attorney as well, but not one like you will have."

"Some of the things on this list, I'm assuming." She only nodded. Storm wasn't going to tell him what else they'd been able to find but decided to let him hear about it when the time was better. "May I ask about Georgie?"

"Yes. But you're not going to like it any more than I did. Mom was notified two weeks ago that Georgie passed away in his sleep. He was in poor shape when Rain and I found out about him several months ago. We'd been making sure he had better care, but it was simply too much for him. They told me when I asked that he'd lived a great deal longer than they ever thought he should have."

Storm let her dad cry. She hadn't known about her brother until recently, but it had still hurt her and Rain when they heard about his passing. Dad told her he'd not known that he'd died, and that hurt him as well. He told her it saddened him too that he had no memories of him that he could tell her about.

"Georgie hadn't ever been where he could come home to stay with us. I went to visit him daily for a while. Then your mom—well, it was easy for her to convince me that seeing him was a waste of time, as he didn't know anything." Dad seemed to be coming to terms with other things as well. "After you and Rain were born, there was a time when I thought of leaving her. I know I should have, but she said she'd sell the two of you off to some pervert, and I'd never see you again. I believed her then, and I believe to this day she would have done so. If for no other reason than to have taken someone else from me."

"Dad, she's talking to the police about how you made her have a handicapped child for the extra money. The man working for you on this said it wasn't a possible excuse for her to use because there hadn't ever been a question of money given to you after he was born." Dad said that was cold of her. "I'm beginning to think she's been cold and manipulative for a very long time."

"She killed her parents too." That Storm hadn't known and told her dad that. "Linda told me it had been an accident that night, but I never really believed her. So one night, I got on the Internet and did some checking around. She'd driven over them when she was pulling into the garage and said she'd not seen them. Why she was driving the car at all at her age isn't something that I've ever been able to figure out. Her father was a huge man from the pictures I've seen. Unless he was laying on the floor when she drove up and over him, there wasn't any way she couldn't have seen him. Your grandmother lived, but she had such severe brain damage that soon after that, she was taken off life support. Linda told me she was about fifteen when it happened, but she was younger. About eight or so, according to the articles I read. Now that I've had time to think about it, I do believe she was the age she told me. At eight, she might not have been able to reach the pedals or have the knowledge to do that sort of horrific thing. But then, who knows with her."

After that, they only talked about what was going to happen to him. She thought her dad had come to the realization that Mom wasn't a nice person from the very beginning of her life and only dragged him along because she'd found someone she could make do what she wanted when she wanted it.

Leaving the jail after visiting her father, she went to find Edwin, who was working in the same house as the rest of the family, on a few projects about another building they all owned. This house, their main location, was an old Victorian house that she loved, and since they'd never done anything to it, she thought it would make a nice house again. Maybe she'd talk to Edwin about it sometime.

"There you are." She smiled when he kissed her despite his brothers making fun of him. "I have something I'd like for you to look over. I've been thinking about the things Romeo was telling me about that he didn't get around to setting up, and I was wondering what you thought about working on them now."

"You mean working on the after-school program." He nodded and showed her what he'd been thinking about. "This isn't going to work. For one thing, it's much too far away from the school for kids to be going there. Secondly, it's too close to the bar. Even though it's not open and running now, it might reopen someday, and that would be bad for kids."

She helped him with a couple more projects, then said she was going to talk to his brothers. Tony and Jeffery had a separate building in the area that they worked from, and that was where they were now with Rain. Sitting down across from Luna before leaving, the older woman asked her why she was waiting to talk about the building they were currently in. Storm wasn't the least bit surprised that she knew, either.

"You're established here. You've been working here, I bet since this place was built." Luna pointed out that they'd outgrown it, the reason two of her sons had moved out. "Will you want to work all together again? I mean, no offense, but it gets really crowded in here at the best of times. What do you do when you have to gather together?"

"We go to one of the houses. And I believe the house you and Edwin are in now would be suitable for your sister and Paul. You two would be well served to live in this house. Edwin would love it as well." She said she hadn't any idea. "You will come to realize that Edwin will do anything to make you happy. But in this, he has forever loved this house. And when he was looking for a place to live, I thought for sure he'd ask us to move out of here so he could."

"Will you?" Luna said she'd gladly do that, but she'd have to help her find a place for them to work from. "I think, after only spending a few hours here, you'd be better served, as you called it, to work from separate buildings too. You nearly walk over each other now, and I don't think it has anything to do with the lack of space. All of you want to be involved in what the other is doing. That makes for poor workmanship. I bet Tony and Jeffery get more done in one day than you guys do in a week."

"Yes, now that you mention it." She looked around. "Most of the time, one or two of them are in here with me, helping me go over contracts and such. I had to learn to read when they did. Being a wolf, I didn't know a great many things that come naturally to human children. They've gotten into the habit of helping, and it never went away."

"Nah. They love being around you. I do as well. You give off an energy that seems to make people want to be near you. I thought it was the wolf part of you, but I think now that it's because you're simply a wonderful person, human or wolf." Luna thanked her. "No need for that. I'm hoping you'll teach me to be a kinder person. I'm much too blunt for people. And when I try to be nice, they seem to think I'm waiting to stab them in the back with something."

"You do give off the vibe of not trusting too much." They both laughed again. "I'll look into buildings around here with you, and we'll get them moved out so you can get inside this house. You'll not change it around much, will you?" Storm told her she saw no reason to do that as they'd added what she'd need to make it a nice, comfy home. "I have things for you too that were Edwin's. Each son had their own baby bed made by the craftsmen of the pack. They're beautifully made, and there are other things with them. Handmade blankets and such. I'll sort them out as soon as we get the buildings squared away."

"Thank you. We're going to have children, and I'm looking forward to that." Luna said she was as well. "I bet you are."

She and Luna visited several buildings around the town. Two of them weren't fit to be standing, so they made notes to have them torn down. Luna was well liked around town, and she introduced her to everyone they encountered. There were people thanking her for her help on different projects around town too. As soon as they found the third building, one that would work for her and Charlie, they decided to have a little snack to tide them over until dinner. Rain joined them when they were just sitting down.

"There are two things I'd like to cover with the two of you. One of them is the housing issues we're having around here. I know there are a great many rentals, but maybe you can tell me why these people are living in slums when there is a perfectly good hotel that can be used for them that would suit them better." Luna asked for more details, and Rain had them. "Most of the elderly have been tossed aside, at least that's what it looks like to me. But even with that, there are a few families that could use a good hand up as well. I don't mean jobs, not right this minute. It's difficult to be able to hold down a job when you have nowhere to get ready for it. But housing would be my next step in getting this place up and going again. It's sort of running on empty."

As they talked about things they could do, Storm was happy that Luna treated her sister as if she were one of her children too, scolding her when she seemed to be putting herself down and praising her when she had a good idea. And Rain had a great many of them. She thought that with the help of the other two women and the ones that would join them, the place they called home would be better than ever. Storm couldn't wait to talk to Edwin about all the things that were going to be going on soon. And their new home.

~*~

Tony wasn't entirely sure what he was looking at on the computer until the camera seemed to adjust itself. While he knew what building he was looking at, he had no idea why it had been important for him to get up in the middle of another project and see what was going on with this camera. Watching the camera go back and forth, he noticed that at some point in its turn, something had happened. Zooming in was difficult, as he had to wait for the camera to adjust, but he soon realized he wasn't going to be able to see anything unless he went to the scene he was trying to look at.

"I can help you with that, my lord." He didn't even look when someone spoke beside him but moved over so that the small one could help. A great many things had been going on over the last few days, and to him, this was just one more thing he was going to have to get used to. "My name is Snowflake. The camera, I believe, is too old for this computer. Let me fix that for you."

The computer was old, but he'd not replaced it simply because it still worked. But the moment Snowflake touched the housing unit, he could see a marked difference in the way it worked. Moving the camera so it stayed still on the figure he could now see, he asked Snowflake if he knew anything about him.

"I know she is not a him." He only glanced at Snowflake when she laughed. "I know that for some time now, she's been hiding in that alley to see if she could get something to eat for herself and her little boy. He is a good lad, this child of hers. I don't know why she isn't living with his father, but then I've only been watching her for a couple of days."

"Does she seem to be a good mom?" He laughed. "Never mind. I would have to think she is, or she'd not be getting food out of the dumpster there for them to eat. It takes a brave woman to—is that him?"

"Yes. The little boy. As you can see, he is the watcher for her as she gets them something to eat. I think her to be about Lady Storm's age. The boy, he might be as old as six or younger. Would you like to go there and meet them? I can arrange it." Watching them both, he asked Snowflake if she thought that was a good idea.

"I would think you going there to meet them would be better than them living off the streets. A bed and a good meal would go a long way for them both, don't you think?"

"Yes, you're right." As he was getting up to go, he noticed another figure creep into the camera's view. "Who is that?"

"I don't know, my lord. I shall go there now and meet you there. Oh my, he's taking the child."

Tony left his house without thought to what he might encounter when he got to them. All he knew was that he had to be there to make sure they were both safe.

He could have run to the place as his wolf, but he knew if he had to bring them back with him, he'd need his car. Tony had to concentrate on driving safely all the way there. As soon as he got out of his car, he saw the man coming out of the alley with the child over his shoulder, screaming to be let go, and the woman being dragged out by her hair. Since she wasn't saying anything to her treatment, Tony figured she was either dead or unconscious.

"What the hell do you think you're doing?" The man nearly dropped the boy when he startled him. "You should really let them both go, or I'm going to kill you. I'm not going to tell you a second time."

"Really. Well, I got news for you, you fucking dick, she's my wife, and she's run off for the last time with my kid here." Tony asked him if he thought her running off had anything to do with his treatment of her. "What business is it of yours? I told you she's my wife, and I'm going to do with her what is necessary to keep her in line."

"No." He felt relief all through his body when Edwin spoke behind him. "You'll release them both right now, or so help me, the police will never be able to pick up all the pieces of you to have someone identify you when you're dead. And you will be if you don't give that little boy to my brother and let the woman go."

Tony hadn't contacted his family when he'd left his work, but he was glad they were with him. Just knowing that all five of them had come to help made him feel like this was the right thing to do.

The man tossed the boy at him, and it was only by pure instinct that he caught him before he could hit the ground. But when he turned to— Tony thought—hurt the woman, the low growl had him pausing in mid-kick to her belly.

"I told you there would be no second chances with this. Drop her or die." The man let her hair go, and Snowflake appeared. She disappeared again with the woman, and he was glad for her help. "Get out of here while you still can."

The man bumped him as he walked by. Tony, again relying on his forethought, clawed at the man deep enough to draw blood. Taking it to his mouth as the man watched, Tony watched the man with horror written all over his face.

"Edwin, he's a wolf."

That was all it took for his brother to shift and kill the man. There was no tolerance for harming a child that was your own. It was worse when you harmed your mate. It was a death quicker than he would have given him, and Tony was glad that Edwin had done it rather than him. Edwin had torn his throat out. Tony was sure he would have made him suffer a great deal more.

"Where is my mom?" Tony had completely forgotten about the little boy. He told him she was safe. "She needs me."

"Yes, of course, she does. Come on, we'll go to the hospital and make sure you're both all right." He laid his head on his shoulder, and Tony looked at his brothers. "Thank you for this.

I don't know who contacted you, but I'm so glad you were here."

"Snowflake did. She is a good person to have around." Edwin had changed back to himself and was dressed as well by then. Jeffery and the others were going to go with him to the hospital, and he was also glad for that. "She's at the hospital now. When she arrived at our home, Storm called an ambulance for her. She said she'd meet us there."

On the way there, he held onto the little boy. He alternated between hugging him tightly, thanking him for saving him, and crying softly about his mom. Tony asked him for his name and was told that he was a stranger. It was funny, really, that he'd say that. After saving his life and that of his mother, holding him to make sure he was comforted, the little fellow still thought of him as a stranger.

"Have you given any thought to what she might be to you?" Tony asked Edwin what he meant. "I don't know, Tony. Your mate? Could that be why you needed to be here?"

"I never really gave it much thought, to be honest with you." He tightened his grip on the little boy when he cried out in his sleep. "I don't think it would be such a heartache to have her in my heart. Nor this little man."

"I'm glad to hear you say that. She is, by the way. Your mate. The boy will become your son. I wanted you to know that in the event you decide to walk away when she wakes. I'm to understand from Storm that she's not too terribly trusting of people. And she'll be less so when it comes to having you being a wolf."

"I'll just have to work harder in convincing her, I guess. Love her for sure, but make sure she hasn't any doubt that I'll never harm her. She should never have been treated this way from the beginning." They pulled up in front of the hospital then, and neither of them moved. "Ask Storm for me if I should allow the boy to see his mom before he's looked over. I'm assuming she's with her."

"She is, and I've asked. Storm said his mom is in surgery right now. She was beaten up badly." Nodding, neither of them moved. "It'll be all right, Tony. You will convince her, I'm sure of it."

"Magically sure, or just sure?" He told him he had all the faith in the world in him. "Thank you for that. I think I might need it."

They went into the emergency room, and he was taken back with the little boy as soon as they were in the big area. Lying him gently on the bed, he held onto his hand while the nurses prepped him for some tests. It was going to be a long wait, and he was glad that his family, his parents included, showed up too.

"She's going to be all right, son." Tony told his dad he hoped so. "You believe in it. The moment you came into their lives, they were immortal. That will go a long way in keeping them both from too much more harm. You must believe that."

"I do." He told his dad he'd not gotten to say much to either of them. "She was unconscious when I arrived, and the little guy was already in the man's clutches."

"I know them, or at least their names, but I'll not tell you unless you ask. They'll both need trust, and knowing more about them than they'll share with you will make it more difficult for them to believe you have their best interest at heart." Tony agreed with his dad. "The little boy means I have a grandson. You've no idea how that makes this old man feel."

They were still talking about the newest additions to the family when the doctor came to talk to them about the little man. It was difficult for him to allow him to go without him to get scme tests run. After about ten minutes of them being gone, a nurse asked him to come with her. Apparently, he was begging for Tony to come to be with him, and he couldn't have been happier.

AWARD WINNING, BESTSELLING AUTHOR

Kathi Barton, a winner of the Pinnacle Book Achievement Award and a best-selling author on Amazon and All Romance books, lives in Nashport, Ohio, with her husband, Paul. When not creating new worlds and romance, Kathi and her husband enjoy camping and going to auctions. She can also be seen at county fairs with her husband, who is an artist and potter.

Her muse, a cross between Jimmy Stewart and Hugh Jackman, brings her stories to life for her readers in a way that has them coming back time and again for more. Her favorite genre is paranormal romance, with a great deal of spice. You can visit Kathi online and drop her an email if you'd like. She loves hearing from her fans. aaronskiss@gmail.com.

Follow Kathi on her blog: http://kathisbartonauthor. blogspot.com/

www.ingramcontent.com/pod-product-compliance
Lightning Source LLC
Chambersburg PA
CBHW030224180626
46810CB00008B/2952